Pick Your

Jayne Rylon

Pick Your Pleasure
Jayne Rylon

Published by Jayne Rylon

Copyright 2012 Jayne Rylon
Edited by Chloe Vale
ISBN: 978-0-9888124-1-3

Dedication

For my brother, Kolin, and his friends, who texted from a bar in NYC with a great (I hope) idea for my next book…

Also to Lexi Blake for encouraging me to experiment. I appreciate all your help in getting me off the ground and the fact that you accept payment for your shared wisdom in the tender of sexy pictures of men.

None of this would have been possible without Chloe Vale. Thank you, thank you, thank you!

To find out more about how *Pick Your Pleasure* works, please visit JayneRylon.com.

Underground

"It's been a pleasure," Linley Lane lied.

She pasted on her diplomatic smile as she allowed her date to buss her cheek and politely shake her hand as they parted ways on the red carpet of the valet portico outside L'Etoile.

Another miserable date.

That was probably harsh. It had been blah.

Make that at least sixty-two in a row. Or was it sixty-three?

Sure, Paolo had given her eyes plenty to feast on during the dinner they'd shared. His intelligence, along with genuine Italian features, olive skin, and his sexy accent should have been enough to make any woman swoon. Plus, his family's shipping empire ensured his interest had more to do with her personally than the fortune she'd amassed by building her application development business from the ground up.

But there simply hadn't been any chemistry between them.

Not a single firework.

Or even a spark.

Not a glimmer of lust had fluttered her stomach when he'd dusted a kiss over her knuckles before dessert. It hadn't taken her more than a moment's hesitation to decline his offer of after-dinner drinks—at his place, or hers, or the ritzy hotel across the street.

Hell, the fact that she'd entertained the notion even that long when he didn't have the *it* factor she searched for could only mean she was getting desperate.

Finding a guy was hell when the most attractive thing about you seemed to be the hundreds of millions you'd

5

banked by being savvy, refusing to quit, and working your ass off. She'd waited so long to get in the game, focused on work instead of socializing, that she admitted she probably didn't know how to date like most women her age.

By thirty-three, she should have some skills, know how to take a man home for a night of fun, or play the seductress in a drawn-out affair. Instead, she probably conducted her rendezvous more like interviews for a mate.

On paper, her recent dates looked like perfect matches. And not a single one of them had given her any sort of zing. Success hadn't come without roadblocks. If nothing else, she'd learned to problem solve like a beast. She needed a new approach.

Time for Plan B.

Drawing her pre-release prototype phone—which had been issued by the testing team of a leading cell manufacturer—from her purse, she traced the symbol that would quick dial Henry as she approached her car.

"Everything all right, Linley?" Her head of security answered before the damn thing had even buzzed once. "Your date…?"

"It's a bust. Nothing's wrong other than my old-maid status." She sighed. That certainly wouldn't cause her personal injury unless she gouged her eyes out or died of sexual starvation. Her security detail got nervous when she insisted they stay at home, so what she was going to ask next would probably blow the top of his head off. She didn't care. "Henry?"

"Yeah." His gruff response made it clear he understood he wasn't going to like this call.

"Tell me the name and address of the club you visit when you need something…adventurous."

"Linley?" He tried to pull his silent-but-strong-type bullshit on her. Fooling her would take more than that.

"Do you really think I'd hire you without snooping into

your private life at least half as much as you did into mine?" She laughed.

"I wouldn't respect you if you hadn't." He grunted. "But I thought you had more tact than to mention my playground after all these years. Why don't I come over and we can discuss—?"

"No." She knew he didn't intend it as a come on. They'd worked together for nearly a decade. They didn't have the spark either, though her head bodyguard could make any number of women praise the male gender. "You're not going to sway me. Just give me the damn information, and don't butt in."

"You're serious?" He paused, as if he was holding the phone away from his face so she wouldn't catch his cursing.

"Will I be safe there?" She doubted he'd visit a place where women weren't respected.

"Damn it, Linley." He blew out a puff of air then reconsidered. "Yes. No one will hurt you at Underground. There are rules. I'll call the owner—"

"No. I want to go to a place where no one knows who I am. Somewhere I can be a random woman out to have fun and hook up." She pinched the bridge of her nose. "Just for tonight. Let me have that."

"You won't be able to get in if I don't pull a few strings," he insisted. "Usually a member has to apply for a trial then escort a new recruit."

"Fine. Do whatever it takes. Will my car be okay there? Or should I go home and take a taxi?" She triggered the ignition of her Alfa Romeo 8C Competizione with a new phone app they were working the bugs out of, loving the roar of the engine. If they could get it to work on something as finicky as her car, they could make it work for everyone. She tossed her cell to the bucket seat beside her as it automatically flipped to hands-free mode.

"You can park in the subterranean garage. Your baby

will have good company down there. The club takes all types, Linley." Henry's resigned report accompanied the tapping of keys. "I'm sending a navigation map to your car now. I've already texted the owner to let him know you're on your way."

"Thanks, Henry." She drummed her fingers on the steering wheel. No backing out now.

"You know, you *can* change your mind. Or just go to have a couple of drinks. If it's not for you, head out. Call me if you'd like me to come get you." His offer muted when he must have covered the receiver with his hand for a bit. A murmured apology caught her attention.

"You've got someone with you tonight," she whispered. Jealousy turned her an unattractive shade of green. Not for his hot body, but for the ease with which he was able to find women to keep him company. The power of her position often intimidated men and kept them from approaching her. "Sorry, Henry. I shouldn't have bothered you on your night off. You take so few."

"It's fine." His warm voice made his smile evident even over the phone. "You deserve to blow off some steam, too. Hope you realize how much *fun* you could be in for. Almost wish I could see your face..."

"I'm not a prude, you know." She snorted.

"You've never been to a place like Underground before." He seemed so smug, she doubled her determination to prove him wrong.

"I can handle myself." If she weren't zipping along the highway ramp, she might have crossed her arms over her chest.

"I know you can. That's the only thing that convinced me to make this connection for you." Henry probably rolled his eyes like he did when he thought she couldn't see. "I only have a job if you're around, kid."

She laughed. "Always the practical one. Thanks, Henry.

Get back to your *friend*."

"Yes, ma'am." He paused before disconnecting. "You're going to have the wild night you're craving, boss. Just...pick your pleasures wisely."

Before she could ask what he meant by that, he'd severed the connection, probably to dive beneath the covers with his woman of the moment again. Too bad there hadn't ever been any sparks between her and Henry. Loyal, handsome, and funny—he'd make someone a kickass husband someday.

If he ever decided to settle down.

Linley shook her head. It hadn't been until the last year or so that the idea of meeting a man and maybe having a family had taken center stage in her mind. All through her twenties, she'd focused on building her empire. And now that she ruled her own world, she'd found it could be lonely at the top.

She glanced at the glowing line in her customized dash. Only three more miles to the club. Shifting gears, she set her baby to cruise while she drew her diamond necklace over her head then shook off her matching bangle. The silk scarf she'd dressed up her black bandage dress with came next. She tucked the valuables in the special safe in the glove box then ruffled her hair, loosening the long waves from the updo she'd pinned them into.

Smudging her makeup a bit added a smoky haze around her steel-gray eyes. "You'll do," she told herself.

Heartbeat steady, breathing slow and deep, she turned into the discreet garage her car instructed her to occupy. A man in a suit met her at the booth. He waited patiently with his hands folded in front of his waist as she parked in the spot he indicated.

When she slid from her car, he approached.

"Ms. Lane." He nodded.

"Good evening." She pretended she had clandestine

interludes with strangers who knew her all the time. It was either that or kick start her encounter on an awkward footing.

Losing this thrill, the anticipation of a reckless moment, didn't interest her. Not when she'd fought so long to find it. Had running her own company turned her into an adrenaline junky? Maybe.

Tonight she'd find a rush one way or another.

"Henry spoke well of you." The gentleman didn't lead her into the building just yet. "We have high standards here at Underground. Please understand that there are rules you will need to follow if I take you farther."

"And they are?" She refused to fidget, meeting his assessing gaze head on.

"If you had agreed straight off, without asking, I'd have sent you home. So, congratulations. You're off on the right foot." His mouth tipped up at one corner. "Inside there is a lot of…variety. Judgment has no place here. If what you're shown is not the pleasure you seek, keep going. Pick something else. No one is to be demeaned for their selection."

"Of course." She nodded. What kind of asshole did they think she was anyway?

"At Underground, all that matters is the moment. Don't ask questions. Who? What? Why? Irrelevant. People come here to escape. We can guarantee you that no one is married, or at least not present without the consent of their spouse. Our screening ensures this as well as the health of our members. Henry forwarded me your files. You're clear."

"Wow." She had no idea how he'd done that, but it shouldn't have surprised her. As for the rest, it was better than she could have hoped. Lies wouldn't be necessary to evade questions about her job.

Damn, Henry had been holding out on her all this time.

Underground could be everything she needed.

"Finally, what happens here stays here."

"Like Vegas." She grinned.

"Exactly." Her welcoming committee joined her. His stunning smile had her realizing just how handsome he was beneath his cool, collected exterior. "But better. So much better."

"So, what're we waiting for?" Linley strode toward him and he pivoted, extending his arm. She threaded her hand through the space between it and his solid torso, her fingers landing on the crook of his elbow. The support was appreciated. Between her high heels and the shivers of excitement now racking her, she leaned on him.

The moment they entered the short hallway and headed into the heart of Underground, Linley realized she hadn't set her expectations high enough. Beautiful people surrounded her, peering at the fresh meat being escorted into their midst.

Lavish furnishings in maroon damask, plus black chandeliers, could have made the place reek of bordello. Somehow it didn't. The sophisticated taste of the pieces ensured they enhanced the sensuality of the environment without tipping into gaudy.

Candelabras illuminated the space with a warm glow that turned marble and velvet into hospitable finishes. If she hadn't been so focused on what awaited ahead, she would have paused to admire the erotic art adorning the walls.

Henry had some explaining to do.

"Ms. Lane." Her guide ushered her into a gathering room. A large one. Fireplaces cast sultry shadows across expansive area rugs. Plush and inviting, she could easily lounge here for a decade or two. Busy observing the mingling couples—or more—she didn't realize the greeter had led her to a secluded corner booth with an ornate silver table in the center.

A bottle of champagne chilled on ice. She recognized the label as a premier vintage. The three glasses surrounding it gave her pause.

Linley looked up to find two men occupying the table. One blond and well kept. The other dark and scruffy.

Manners, or maybe some innate formality on his part, dictated the light-haired gentleman rise. He offered her his hand and helped her get situated in the intimate space. His grip was warm and strong. Who was he? Why was she drinking with him and his friend?

As if her greeter could sense the uncertainty swirling around her brain, he explained. "You'll require a guide for your adventure tonight. New members are always paired with a veteran on their first go around to ensure their enjoyment."

"I thought that was your job?" She tipped her head as she examined his expression.

"I wish I were so lucky." He gave her a tiny bow. "Chase and Ryder have both offered their company this evening. We'll leave the choice to you. Play nice, boys."

The greeter winked at her before retreating, perhaps to collect another very willing guest from the garage.

"So long as I don't have to fight fair." The bump on scruffy guy's nose attested to his experience with brawling. She felt bad for prince charming across the table if things came to blows.

"Wouldn't expect you to, Ryder." The burnished blond shook his head though he smiled as he said it.

Dashing, dangerous, and devilish, Ryder scooted closer and laid his palm high on her thigh. Entirely too close to the hem of her dress for someone she hadn't even officially been introduced to yet.

Denying the electricity his skin conducted would have been pure insanity. Hot and firm, his touch did things to her she'd never imagined possible with a single contact. He didn't wait for her approval or shrink from her—Linley Lane, CEO.

Was it like this for other women? Or was this man something special?

A tiny connection and he did more for her than the parade of perfect men who'd come before him. She blew out a sigh that ruffled her bangs, washing her cheeks with a cool breeze.

"Hands off my lady, please." Chase didn't seem disturbed by the zero-to-a-million-and-sixty approach Ryder adopted with her. His quiet confidence made her do a double take at his model good looks. Hell, he had most of Hollywood beat in her book.

Piercing blue eyes met her curious stare. He didn't flinch from her inspection. Patient yet persistent, he waited for her to look her fill. With thick lashes and a couple of laugh lines that hinted at a good nature, she hoped she wasn't drooling.

What were the odds? Two men. Both of whom she had compelling—if completely opposite—chemistry with.

Hot damn.

Linley licked her lips.

"Would you care for a drink?" Chase's smooth baritone made her blink twice before she deciphered his offer.

"Yes, please." She studied his expert handling of the bottle, impressed with how he poured the crisp liquid without spilling a single bubbly drop. When she reached for the stemware he proffered, he surprised her by clasping her fingers in a gentle yet sure hold then dusting the back of her hand with his lips.

A tantalizing appetizer.

Before she could dig in, he slipped the glass into her hand and wrapped her fingers around the delicate crystal.

"What century are you from?" Ryder growled as he ignored his rival to focus on her. "Either way, you'll be ancient before you get to the good shit with him."

The rebel's fingers hadn't moved from her leg. Well, maybe they had. Higher.

Instead of creeping her out, his deft massage encouraged Linley to sink into the tufted velvet, allowing her thighs to relax and part. Just a bit.

"You didn't come here tonight to be bored, did you?" Ryder reached across her to cup her cheek in his broad, slightly callused hand while the other continued to mesmerize her with his intuitive knowledge of her erogenous zones. Nudging her chin up, he forced her to meet his gaze. His fingers curled around her nape, and he leaned forward until his lips nearly collided with hers. "Pick me. I'll make sure you never forget the night you decided to be a bad girl."

When she nearly succumbed to the promise of his slightly rough cheek to steal a kiss, he retreated, though his skilled fingers continued their insidious assault.

"I hardly call romance dull." Chase sipped from his glass, reminding her of the treat fizzing away before her.

Linley downed a swallow or two. Moisture gathered at the corner of her mouth. Before she could reach for her napkin, Chase swiped a droplet from her lips with his thumb then sampled the mingled flavor of the alcohol and her skin.

"Delicious." He savored the taste and looked like he might go for another.

She wished he would. Instead he withheld the pleasure, making her yearn for more.

A glint from Ryder's direction had her glancing away in time to see him chug his drink then pour another round. The powerful flex of his throat—primal and strong—inspired her. In her mind, she could picture nibbling the cords there as he rode her. With him, she wouldn't have to beg for what she wanted.

He wouldn't make her take.

So many times, she had to be the aggressor. In meetings. In dating. Handing over the reins would be a welcome relief. This man would afford her that luxury.

When he was down to the last sip of the second round, he held it in his mouth and set his glass on the table with a *clunk*. This time he didn't stop when he swooped in. His lips landed on hers without apology.

Ryder proved that though he might lack stealth, he had finesse in abundance. His mouth turned hers pliant as he shared the rich drink and a taste of what a night with him would be like. He sucked on her tongue, using the slightest edge of his teeth to awaken nerves gone drowsy with an intoxicating blend of allures.

When he withdrew, he bit her lip lightly, letting the subtle sting remind her of the things he'd done to her body without effort. Her nipples rubbed against the padding of her bra. She attempted to cross her legs to appease the part of her that screamed for pressure right where she needed it most.

To her surprise, it was Chase who prevented her from trapping Ryder's palm between her thighs. "No, love. Don't hide. You didn't come here tonight for that."

"And what if I've changed my mind?" Having two men bracketing her, promising her their own brand of sexy fun, overwhelmed her. For a moment, she wondered if she could handle it. Or would she disappoint them? It wasn't like she had a ton of experience.

"Then let me take you home." Chase's solution seemed genuine. "That's not code for anything, by the way. I'll drop you at your door, safe and sound, if you'd prefer."

"No one's forcing her." Ryder seemed offended. "But I won't let you lie to yourself, wildcat. You came hunting for this. You're soaked. My finger isn't sliding around on its own down there. I'll make it easy for you, give you things you never dreamed you needed."

Linley's head *thunked* against the seat as she dropped it backward. "Too bad I can't have you both."

Ryder laughed. The easy, boisterous sound made it clear he did it often. With gusto. "In my world, that's an option. Here we're Underground. The next level below us is called Downstairs. I hang out a bit deeper. The Basement of the club offers the possibility of ménage, among other more daring pursuits. Chase doesn't sink that low, though."

She peeked up in time to catch the other man's tiny frown.

"That's true," Chase confirmed. "I prefer to stick to Downstairs. And I fly solo. I assure you, you won't need other men when you have my full attention. For dipping your toe in, I recommend the first level of the club. Perfect for wading."

"Screw that. Jump into the deep end." Ryder lifted his palm from her saturated thigh, licked his finger, and then held out his hand. "I won't let you drown."

"Neither will I." Chase extended one of his as well.

"So, who will it be, Linley?" She didn't have time to wonder how they knew her name.

Instead she searched inside and uttered her preference for tonight.

If Linley said *Chase,* turn to page 59, *Linley Picked Chase.*

If Linley said *Ryder,* turn to page 80, *Linley Picked Ryder.*

Play Downstairs

"I saw plenty to keep me busy up here." A sigh of relief passed her lips when he didn't seem in the least disappointed. "Hell, yes." He hugged her to him and laid a wet kiss on her lips. "I probably couldn't have controlled myself long enough to show you around the Basement properly tonight. I would have done my best. But you're firing me up, Linley."

"I'll take a rain check." Was it okay to suggest they might play again someday? She hoped so. Now that she'd discovered this incredible chemistry, she had no delusions that one night—however insanely good it was—would be enough.

"You got it." Ryder nodded. "Anytime."

"So how do these rooms work?" She lifted her chin toward the one on the end marked Ties That Bind.

"See the little red light?"

Linley nodded.

"That means it's occupied. If you're interested, we'd tell one of the servers to put us on the waiting list. You can specify a room—the popular ones have a couple of spares around the backside—or ask for the next available if you're feeling lucky...or horny." He gave his cock a few tugs as if to settle himself. She swallowed hard. "Once the players are finished and the room is cleaned and reset, someone will notify us."

"I see." Damn it, both of the possibilities she'd fantasized about forever had a red light on their doors.

"Why? Do you know what you want already?" He narrowed his eyes.

"Yes, I think so." She bit her lip, wondering if she could stand the delay or if she should settle for something else.

Anything would do as long as her date administered corresponding pleasure. Soon she wouldn't be able to stand for the desire pulsing through her core.

Ryder snagged a passing dude. The guy was built like a football player yet moved with nimble strides. "The lady would like to reserve a room."

When she opened her mouth to put in her request, Ryder held out his hand with one finger up and the rest curled into a fist. "Hang on."

Her order died in her throat. Had he changed his mind? Did he want to set their course? She wouldn't mind giving him full control once inside, but picking the room allowed her to put some boundaries in place.

"No, no." He shook his head after taking one peek at her crestfallen face. "Not what you're thinking. Just… Why don't you whisper your selection to Robbie? I'm kind of a sucker for surprises. Spontaneity. I don't want to know until we're crossing the threshold what the night has in store for us. Besides, I might not be able to contain myself. I can be impatient on occasion."

The server chuckled. "You're not usually one of the guys who ends up fucking his date against the wall then heading home without enjoying the finer pleasures we have to offer. It's kind of nice to see someone giving as good as they get with you, Ry."

Ryder flipped the guy off. "Go ahead, tell the smartass your choice so we can take care of some business. I might succumb tonight. If I do, though, I swear there's more waiting for you, Linley. You're not leaving here tonight less than totally satisfied. If we have to get someone from the Basement to help, we will."

"Thanks, but I have no doubts you're going to rock my world." It was a given. He already had. She didn't know if anything could ever live up to this. Tonight might very well be the highlight of her sex life. Then what?

"And what room is he going to do that in, sweetheart?" The server leaned down so she could reach his ear. It felt odd to be surrounded by men and not have her power heels on. Or her business suit. Or any kind of pants at all for that matter. Linley whispered her selection into his ear.

"Very nice." Robbie winked at her. "He'll adore accommodating your desires."

"I hope so," she muttered as the man returned to his post and tapped their request into the computer stationed there.

"Enough of that, wildcat." Ryder cupped her cheek in his palm and angled her face toward him. "I'll enjoy this as much as you do. I bet you're stunning when you come apart."

What the hell was the heat flashing across her cheeks? A blush! She hadn't done that since she was a preteen, she was sure.

"Until our room is ready, let's see how bold you can be." Ryder led her to the lounge area. She realized now it was more than a simple waiting room or a mingle zone.

The visual stimulation provided by couples engaging in full-on intercourse—right in the open where others could observe—had her rocking backward. Certainly not in disgust either.

"You like the idea?" He brushed her hair off her shoulder then dropped light kisses on the bare skin there.

"Mmm." She glanced over her shoulder. "There's something about the pride it takes to show off like that. Both in yourself and your partner."

"Yeah." He grunted. "I totally agree. And I'm willing to make every man in this room jealous that I have you to myself tonight. Even if I let them have a peep or two of how spectacular you're going to be."

"How do you know that?" She worried about the level of experience a lot of these patrons clearly had that she didn't.

"Because I can see it in your eyes. You wouldn't have come here tonight if you didn't have it in you. Maybe your inner vixen took a while to present itself but…you need this. Tonight. Maybe forever after. You do realize that's a risk, right? Getting hooked on the adrenaline high this place can give you?"

"Is that why you come?" she wondered out loud before considering what barriers she might have crossed.

"I'm not sure." He scrubbed his hand over his scruffy jaw. "I think I might have kept my platinum membership status because I was searching for something I hadn't found yet. Fun and fucking occupied me for a while. Tonight is different, Linley. It's more intense. And that's saying something—trust me."

She nodded, unsure of what to say. After all, it was her first time. Of course it felt surreal and powerful to her. The lust pumping through her had smashed the ceiling of her prior encounters almost from the first instant he'd laid his hand on her thigh less than five seconds after being introduced.

Linley couldn't take much more without some relief. The pressure between her legs, in her breasts, and deep inside her soul began to overwhelm her logic. For a levelheaded businesswoman, it was disturbing. And a wonderful rush.

Ryder was right. She could easily become obsessed with this. With him.

Was that the biggest mistake of her life?

"Let me take the edge off for you." He brushed aside her long waves to kiss the nape of her neck. "I'll have enough time to get you back in the game for the main event, I promise."

"Here?" she squeaked.

"Why not?" He shuffled until he stood behind her. His arms wrapped around her waist for a brief hug before roaming across her body from her stomach to her hips to her breasts to the moist panel of lace over her waxed mound. "Like you said, it's a compliment. One I'd like to pay you.

I'm damn lucky to be the guy escorting you tonight. I know it, and I'd love to rub it in just a little."

Linley laughed. She loved the way he could deflect her insecurity and ensure she enjoyed their time together. He had skills. Truth be told, she couldn't wait another moment to see them in action. The slide of his taut pecs and solid abs on her back didn't convince her otherwise.

She craned her neck, and he got the point. Of course he did. He read her like no one else had in her life. Thankfully that included her competitors. If she'd been this transparent in her negotiations, she'd never have made it as far as she had to date.

Ryder's mouth crushed onto hers, making her legs wobbly even as he supported her in the cradle of his arms, which wrapped around her like the world's loveliest boa constrictor. Corded muscles held her up as if it were no effort at all.

Meanwhile, his lips encouraged her to blank out their surroundings and supply her undivided attention to magnifying the passion that coursed through her as he continued to seduce her. Rubs of his lips over hers, the tease of his tongue flicking at the roof of her mouth, and his wandering hands all combined to set her on fire.

While he consumed her, he began to walk them forward. The uncoordinated response of her limbs granted him an excuse to lift her. All she had to concentrate on was the kiss that seemed endless. It intoxicated her with its potency.

Until he broke the contact with a growl that matched her musing on the subject. He paused only long enough to deposit her, supine, on a padded platform at waist height. Not quite a bed, but not a bench either, the furniture had to have been custom made, designed with this purpose in mind.

This place, and the people who owned it, had thought of everything. She silently thanked them for their foresight. Years of trial and error by those who'd come before were paying off, guaranteeing her experience left no room for complaints or improvement.

Soft velvet caressed her back as Ryder's hands glided over her wherever he could reach. "I'm leaving your underwear on. I'd like to save unwrapping that present for myself. Me and only me, okay?"

"Yes." She liked the idea of withholding something for him alone. How could she have met this man less than an hour ago? So little time and already he had her mostly bare, laid out like the main course of some decadent feast.

If she'd known what awaited her tonight, she'd never have found the balls to pull the trigger. Thank goodness for snap decisions with no research to back them up. She didn't utilize that tactic much, but the few times she'd gone with her gut in her life, she'd been rewarded for the risk.

Tonight seemed like no exception.

"That's it, wildcat." Ryder coached her through her revelation. "Relax and let me take care of you. I'll make sure you get what you came for."

"Already have." She reached out to squeeze his thigh. He'd granted her a break from the monotonous series of never-would-be lovers she'd tortured herself with for close to a year. Habits shattered, ruts erased, and bad logic followed by more of the same had finally been circumvented.

"Don't tease me." He shied away from her grip. "I'm on the edge already."

Linley hadn't intended to creep closer to his substantial package, but his warning brought out her naughty side. She slid her fingers higher until they made contact with the soft, roasting flesh between his legs. Curling her hand around his shaft, she measured him once then twice.

Impressive.

Waiting to have him inside her seemed like the dumbest thing she'd ever done. Hopefully the deferred pleasure would make up for the delay.

"If you're not going to listen, I'll have it my way."
Ryder shocked her when he slipped from her grip, moving
quicker than she thought possible. Before she realized what
he intended, he'd rolled her onto her side and stood before
her. The frame of her vision filled with the triangle between
his belly button and the sexy muscles leading at a diagonal
straight to his rock-hard cock.

Her mouth hung open when she got an up close and
personal view. Bigger than she'd realized, he made her
wonder if she could really take all of him.

Ryder didn't waste the opportunity. He fisted his hand in
her hair and thrust his hips forward, prodding at her parted
lips with the blunt cap of his dick. Moisture ensured he slid
across her mouth, adding a gloss to her smile.

"Take a taste," he urged her. "Just a lick or two to hold
you over."

Linley grinned at the roughness in his command. She
gripped his ass with her free arm, and yanked him to her. Her
nails dug into the bunched muscles when he slid inside her
several inches deep.

The taste of him—soap and man—encouraged her to
take another draw. Around her, appreciative whispers
boosted her confidence. When she began to suckle the tip of
Ryder's cock, he withdrew.

"No way are you going to tempt me like that." He
replaced his mouth over hers, sampling their mingled flavors.
When he pulled away, he rested his forehead on hers for a
second as if she'd really made him need to catch his breath.
"I'm not giving in so easily. Though, damn, I wish I were
that kind of guy. You're killing me here, wildcat."

"Know the feeling." She squirmed on the bench, trying
to ignore the crowd gathering around them as if they could
sense the urgency sweeping both her and Ryder into its
grasp. "I need you. Help me."

More complex explanations simply weren't possible.

She allowed her frantic stare to communicate her needs. Fortunately, he understood.

"I've got you." He pressed one last kiss to her lips then rounded the end of the bench. In one lightning move, he'd grabbed her thighs and yanked. Her ass rested on the edge of the platform, on the verge of slipping over, not that he'd allow that to happen.

He cupped her ass and used his shoulders to insinuate his body between her legs.

It wasn't her finest moment, but she whimpered when he dipped low enough to blow a breath over her saturated panties.

And that's when she heard the men who'd ringed them start making wagers. "I bet he can make her come in two minutes or less."

Linley might have laughed. She'd never been one to tip quickly into orgasm. But tonight…well, everything was different. The entire evening had been foreplay, and she felt as though she would shatter at any moment. Each glancing nuzzle of Ryder's face on her mound had her ready to scream.

The guys shook on their gamble. Ryder lifted his head so they could all catch the twinkle in his eyes. "It won't take that long. Give me thirty seconds."

She tried to stop him. He shushed her by placing a love bite on the gentle swell of her belly.

"Don't bother to argue. I'll make you a believer, wildcat." He winked at her then turned to the man beside her shoulder. "Loser pays the winner's membership fee for a year."

"Done." The guy huffed. "You're good, no doubt. Still, she's a first timer. Nervous. I can see it in her hands. They're trembling."

Ryder didn't flinch. Could he know they were shaking because she craved him so badly?

"Then let's get right to it." He nodded to his opponent. "Count it down."

The deceptively respectable-looking man glanced at his Rolex. "Three...two...go!"

Linley braced herself. It didn't matter. He slipped his finger beneath the lace edge and slid the panel to the side, exposing her flesh to his tongue and lips. The initial pressure of Ryder's mouth on her bare pussy had her nearly convulsing.

The appreciative and carnal hum he made as he tasted her for the very first time did more for her than the tame and conscientious caresses of previous lovers. Raw desire had him burrowing deeper into her folds. Despite her attempts to revel in his treatment and the instant, full-speed-ahead pleasure he instilled, the impact he had on her body demonstrated his irresistibility.

"Twenty-five...twenty-six."

The man beside her shouldn't have bothered.

Her capitulation had never been in doubt.

Linley surrendered to the awesome force of the ecstasy Ryder delivered. He pressed a single digit inside her and set her off. She grasped him tight as she rewarded his dexterity and made him a winner. Both of them. Several times over.

And she couldn't wait to do it again.

No lassitude crept over her at the temporary relief. Instead, it flung her higher. If the room didn't free up soon, she'd find out what it was like to fuck in the open. Waiting was no longer an option.

As Linley struggled to rise onto her elbows, a server tapped her on the shoulder. Though not the same man she'd placed her order with, he matched the other in his sexy appeal. Where did they find so many beautiful people? Or was it the libertine attitudes that influenced their appeal and made them so attractive?

She supposed that must be it. Even odder, she figured

she now counted among their ranks considering her pussy still quivered from the aftereffects of Ryder's handling.

Trying for sedate, she couldn't keep herself from bolting to her feet as fast as her liquefied insides would allow. Tugging Ryder, she urged him to hurry. She shouldn't have worried. He clambered beside her. A tiny chink in his feral grace guaranteed the solid erection he sported impaired his typical cool demeanor.

Linley couldn't wait to shatter his self-control. She needed all of him, not some safe version he thought she could handle. The room she'd selected could do that for them both—push them to the cusp and over. If they let it.

Certainty pulsed through her and inspired her wicked smile.

"Damn, wildcat. I like that look. So, where are you taking me?" Ryder's eyes—so brown they were almost black—searched hers. "What room did you ask for?"

"What are *your* favorites?" She hoped they were as compatible as she thought.

"It doesn't matter as long as you're in it. With you, any of the options would be a hell of a lot of dirty fun." The squeeze of his fingers on her reassured her. "But if I had to put something from Downstairs on top of my wish list, it'd either be The Toy Chest or Ties That Bind."

A huge smile planted itself on her face.

"Yeah?" He tugged her closer and swooped in for a relatively quick kiss. Despite its brevity, it sent sparks through her veins. "I'm not surprised we're on the same track. So which one was it?"

If Linley said *The Toy Chest,* turn to page 150, *Ryder Loves The Toy Chest.*

If Linley said *Ties That Bind,* turn to page 164, *Ryder Loves Ties That Bind.*

Fuck Machines Rule

"I'm kind of curious about fuck machines." The admission might have embarrassed Linley earlier in the evening. Any discomfort she'd felt about sharing her desires seemed to have vanished somewhere around the time she'd begged Ryder to fuck her out in the open for everyone to witness.

About then she'd realized she was proud of her passion and the man who managed to magnify its impact on her. Here among others who understood the need for something more than the everyday dating drama—something lustier, something more direct, something darker—for whatever their personal reasons, Linley could be honest.

Ryder had unlocked that capability in her. A huge win, she embraced the change. A million and sixty-two boring dates would never have landed her with the right guy. He'd been waiting here all along.

He turned and called to one of the men in the crowd for assistance.

"Grant, help me get her loose." Her seemingly easygoing guide flashed his inner core of steel. Authority came naturally to him, even if he chose not to employ it most of the time. What did he do to earn that? Where did it come from in real life?

A tendril of recognition stirred within her. Part of her related on a level that insisted he hid a heck of a lot behind his jeans and T-shirt exterior. Or maybe that was her justification for the omissions she'd had to make to follow the rules.

Linley felt off balance, both because of her line of reasoning and because the comfort of her bindings had been stripped away. She tumbled right into Ryder's outstretched arms. He winked down at her as he cradled her against his toasty chest. "Hey there."

"Hi," she whispered with a smile, growing meek just for a moment. It was either that or admit how much more than simply her body was in the game tonight. Foolish to care after a single evening, but she did.

The Basement shifted around her as Ryder toted her to the appropriate portal. She didn't notice much of the surroundings since her stare never wavered from his scruffy jaw. The deep, rich brown of his hair made her long to run her fingers through it, along with the matching trail that lead down his body to his cock.

He gathered her to one side then used his elbow to push the latch-style handle. When he slipped inside, he didn't immediately turn on the lights.

"I'm glad you decided on this room, wildcat." Under cover of darkness, he confessed, "I don't usually mind sharing. Giving my playmate that extra level of pleasure multiple partners can bring is an honor, but something about you has me possessive. I hoped to stake my claim privately before we tried that route."

"I know what you mean." Linley wouldn't deny ménage was a hell of a fantasy. Still, it hadn't tripped her switch tonight. This was about her. And him. And their journey together. "So now that we're alone…what are you going to do about it?"

Ryder's laugh sounded even better with her ear against his chest. He lowered her feet to the floor and kept a steadying hand on her shoulder. Then he began to dial up the dimmer switch. If the outer room of the Basement had piqued her curiosity, the various apparatus sheltered in here had her whistling.

"Holy crap." She stood with her jaw hanging open until Ryder took her fingers in his and led her from station to station. She tilted her head as if looking at some of the contraptions sideways would make their configurations more sensible. "Ryder, I think I'm going to trust you on this one. You're right. Tonight has been damn near perfect. Why stop banking on luck now?"

Black pipes, leather pads, gears, and who knew what else stuck out all over the place.

"Sure thing, wildcat. I know just the thing. But first, come check out your accessory options." Ryder led her to a showcase that was the centerpiece of an entire wall. Glass shelves lit by halogen spotlights made the dildos inside seem like works of art.

"These are all attachments for the machines. Why don't you choose one to get us started?" He gestured to the normal-looking variety on one side and the more outlandish kinds on the other.

Linley glanced down at Ryder's erection.

"You're making me a little self-conscious." He chuckled. "What's with the inspection?"

"I want something close to, but not as good as, the real thing." She smiled up at him. "I assume you're the encore to this experiment?"

"You'd better believe it." He clenched his jaw. "It's hard enough to wait my turn."

"You don't have to if you don't want to." Linley angled her chin toward the enormous bed she'd spotted in the rear of the space. "After everything you've shown me tonight, I think I've realized that having a great time is about the person who takes you on the adventure more than which rabbit hole you fall down."

"Ah, a poet too?" Ryder dipped his head for a kiss. It quickly went from serene to full-octane. "No, wildcat. You're going to get what you came for. And then some."

"I already have." She hugged him tight. "But if you insist…I'll take the model on the second shelf, fourth from the left."

"Good choice." Reaching in the cabinet, he withdrew the dildo that matched his olive complexion. "The veins on this one should work some magic with the machine I had in mind."

"And which one is that?" The throbbing between her legs increased as he hauled her past station after station.

A chair that looked a little too much like a dentist's setup for her peace of mind occupied a corner along with bright lights. A couple with a medical fetish would adore it. Next was a handheld unit on a stand. It looked like it might have once been a reciprocating saw. Then something that seemed to be a fully functioning robotic man. That one gave her the shivers.

She held her breath until they'd crossed almost the entire chamber.

There, at the far end of the bed, something unusual and fun caught her attention. She asked, "This?"

"Mmm." Ryder hummed. "You strike me as the kind of woman who could tame a bucking bronco."

She smiled as she examined the saddle in front of her. Supported on a post, it almost looked like one of those rides she'd seen at the line dancing bar Henry dragged her to on occasion. Except this version had large handrails on either side. They resembled a set of parallel bars with the saddle between them. Affixed to the center of each one was a padded cuff.

When Ryder caught the direction of her gaze, he grinned. "Wouldn't want you falling off and getting hurt now, would we? I have plans to ride you when you're done riding it."

Her knees wobbled at the thought. Their evening had been one long bout of foreplay, and she was eager for the main event.

Ryder caught her and swung her into the saddle. "No

way, wildcat. We're not skipping out on this. I want my show. You realize this room is just as much for the men as the ladies, right? I'm pretty sure I'll never get the image of you on display as you ride this thing out of my mind. Wouldn't want to. I already know it's going to be spectacular."

She bit her lip as she considered performing for him, revving him even higher so that when they finally came together, it was an explosion of passion. A demonstration of what rapture under pressure could do to two people in bed.

"Get your feet in the stirrups." He nudged her legs until they settled into the wooden brackets. Each foothold dangled from a length of leather that Ryder deftly adjusted to the perfect height for her long legs.

For once, she liked how tall she was. He had a good four inches on her nearly six feet. Not a single time during the night had she felt as if she towered over him. Not in stature and certainly not in bearing. He was a welcome relief.

Linley parted her lips to ask him where the dildo he still clutched would come into this equation when he ducked down and fiddled with a panel in her seat. He opened the trap door and attached her selection before buttoning it all up again.

Considering the nature of her business, she could think of a lot of cyber innovations this room would benefit from. Taking in the ones others had dreamed up engaged her mind as well as her body in this quest for relief.

"Ryder. Please hurry." She could hardly believe she'd made it this far without being touched after the close call of the Basement's main area. The urge for something fierce and sudden had banked while she explored. Poised on the cusp of resolution, it returned full force.

"Put your wrists in the cuffs, wildcat." Ryder waited for her to take the initiative and lay her hands inside the wide leather bands. Thankful for the furred interior, she smiled.

31

And when her dream date enclosed her arms—as he had out in the lobby of the Basement—she shuddered.

No panic visited this time. Just instant relief. Their shared bond generated it. She trusted him, and he cared for her. Symbiotic, their exchange sustained them both.

"Lift just a little so I can line you up." Ryder slid his hand between her and the saddle. She realized the padded surface had a square cut in it to allow the dildo to rise and fall from below.

When she posted in the saddle, he triggered the motion of the fucking arm with a small button on the control panel of the machine. The pinpad had been built into one of the arm grip posts. Whoever had designed this contraption had done a lovely job of incorporating all the features a deviant like her would desire.

"Riding lessons were always my favorite, but this has them beat hands down." Linley shuddered when the tip of her selection nudged the inside of her thigh.

"And you haven't seen the best parts yet." Ryder held her as steadily as he could from his position. With his hand still lingering between the leather and her flesh, he guided the faux cock to her pussy as though he were parking an expensive car in a tight space. "Let it settle in before we start playing with the fucking motion.

Linley did as he coached. She gasped when the blunt head of the tool nudged her opening. Then there was no saving her. She sank onto the device, going faster than he'd recommended.

Her wince had him at her side in a flash. He wrapped his arm around her waist and lifted her an inch or so. "What did I tell you about rushing?"

His smack on her ass didn't do much to slow her down.

Linley squirmed in his hold. Relief at finally being filled overwhelmed her. "I'm fine. It's good. So damn great. Let me have it. You."

Pleas rolled off her tongue the instant she admitted that smooth talking wouldn't get her what she wanted this time. "Behave or I'll keep you like this all night." Ryder moaned. "You wouldn't do that to me would you, wildcat?" He took himself in hand and stroked his cock from base to tip several times before abandoning the length, as if afraid of losing his self-control.

"I promise. I'll be good if you give me this cock. And yours right after. Or now. Just...something. Anything."

The raw hunger in his gaze when he stared at her had her on edge.

"Okay. Have it your way. For now, wildcat." He released her, allowing gravity to impale her on the toy. It wasn't until her pussy had settled on the saddle that she realized the nubs on the pommel were ingeniously placed to manipulate her clit.

Ryder smiled at her, the lines of his mouth tight. He sped up the pace of the fucking to something that might not drive her insane in a matter of seconds. Her pussy hugged the toy, wringing it. And just when she was about to ask for more, he pressed another button.

This time it was the saddle that came to life. It rocked her back and forth. The arm of the vibrator stayed in sync with the motion. It kept her filled, or not. The brush of her clit against the enhanced pommel had her calling out to Ryder.

Programming on the machine was top notch. Her company should look into apps for sex toys. She mentally added it to her to-do list.

"Where'd you go, wildcat?" Ryder edged nearer, narrowing his eyes on her. "You're not wandering, are you?"

"Sorry," she apologized. "Just a real life thought that popped into my head. Gone now. Promise."

What did he expect when he scrambled her brain like a chef wielding a whisk?

"You asked for it." He shook his head in mock disapproval then selected another setting. This time the pommel buzzed to life. The devious thing was a vibrator too. *Oh damn.*

Linley leaned forward as if she were jumping gates with one of her horses in the practice ring of her main house's equestrian stables. She didn't give a shit about what she looked like, though the torment on Ryder's face wasn't something he could have faked.

"Grind that pussy on there good and hard." He growled at her as he took himself in hand. "You have no idea how glorious you look. Your long body is stretched out, your hands bound, those legs drawn up and held in pretty stirrups. I can even see the dildo fucking up into you from here."

Adding his heated praise to the sensations bombarding her pushed Linley close to the edge of surrender. Knowing she'd become his center-stage entertainment didn't hurt either. Her entire body quaked as it was shaken, fucked, teased, and filled.

"Come for me, Linley." Ryder used her real name instead of the nickname he'd given her in the first few minutes they'd met. "Show me all you have to give. Then, when I fuck you, right here on the floor, you're going to offer up even more. I know you will."

The dead certainty in his eyes revealed just how powerfully persuasive he could be. Again she wondered at his innate authority. It catapulted her over the edge. She screamed his name as she rode the machine, grinding her pussy on the dildo, the saddle, and the vibrating pommel.

Embarrassment had no place in this ultimate surrender.

Good thing because as she thrashed and groaned, she couldn't have been all that pretty.

Ryder didn't seem to mind. Before she'd truly finished quaking, he'd unhooked her hands, stopped the motion of the various components, and lifted her into his arms once more.

The dildo slipped from her with a decidedly wet noise, accompanied by her groan. "You can play with it more later, if you like. But if I don't have you right now, I'll be spurting on the floor as you enjoy the next temptation."

"I kind of like the idea of that." She gasped as she pictured driving him beyond his iron-fisted control.

"More than the idea of me coming inside you?" He shrugged. "With a condom, of course."

As if he'd reminded himself, he deposited her on a thick area rug piled with pillows then lunged for a nearby chest of supplies.

She almost told him she was on the pill, except he'd already snagged protection, ripped open the packet, and rolled it on his steely length. Waiting another second for him to undo his handiwork didn't appeal. Next time they could negotiate terms like bareback fucking. He'd given her at least some hope there *would* be another rendezvous.

Then all thoughts fled her mind as he stalked back to her and descended, covering her completely with his solid frame. She didn't care if she pouted when she declared, "No more waiting."

"Couldn't agree more." He peppered her with kisses.

Linley drew her knees up beside his trim hips.

He slid in between her thighs. They aligned perfectly without manual intervention. His cock rode the length of her pussy, nudging her clit and causing her to cry out when her lingering orgasm renewed.

Ryder reached between them, pressing down on his cock until the head surged against her saturated opening. He advanced, spreading her far more than the dildo had done. Bigger even than he'd appeared, he filled her completely.

"Yes," she moaned. He matched her groan for groan.

"You're tight, wildcat. Fucking hot around me." He bit her lower lip then began to move. "Need to feel you. Looked so sexy. This time you'll come on me."

She might not have thought she had it in her to crest again so soon, especially not after such an intense experience. Then he slid his hands beneath her and cupped her shoulders, anchoring her against the force of his strokes so he could work himself in her balls deep.

The nudge of his blunt crown against the rear wall of her pussy had her toes curling. She dug her nails into his shoulders and tried to tug him closer, though it would have been impossible for him to fuse them any tighter than they already were.

He ramped up the amplitude and frequency of his fucking, causing her to shiver from the inside out. And just when she thought she might tumble into another epic orgasm, he changed his stride.

Ryder looked down, staring into her eyes. He smiled as he ground them together in a sinful figure eight that sealed their fate.

Linley didn't find words to be necessary. She communicated the impending capitulation of her body with the drum of her heels on his clenching ass.

He nodded at her, giving her permission and promising to accompany her with a single tiny gesture. Stars danced in her vision as she tensed. Probably she should have kept breathing, but everything in her focused on maximizing the pleasure he gave her.

When he leaned forward and bit her neck, all bets were off.

Linley exploded. Her entire body spasmed, milking Ryder's cock.

He shouted her name with each pound of his body within hers. Each pump of his hips came in unison with a pulse of her channel around him. She drew every spurt of his come from his balls with her undeniable ecstasy.

Dazed, she didn't notice when the waves finally stopped battering them, though she registered the floating sensation that accompanied Ryder carrying her to the bed they had been too frenzied to utilize. Ten steps had been too much to contemplate crossing when they'd needed each other so badly. He tucked them beneath the silk sheets together.

Linley smiled and snuggled into his still heaving chest. His fingers tangled in her hair, and he held her close.

To find out what happened next, turn to page 147, *Ryder Epilogue.*

Take Me To The Basement

"I've come this far." Linley gulped. "Take me all the way. I want to see everything. I want to know what it's like to sink to the lowest level."

"I love it when good girls go bad." Ryder looked as though he might have been given the greatest gift of all time or a winning lotto ticket. "*Really* bad."

A tremulous smile crossed her face. She could handle it—him—right?

Kind of too late to run now.

"You've got this." He lead her to the spiral staircase then leaned in to smother her mouth in a ferocious kiss. She allowed him inside, gave him complete possession of her lips and tongue, which he used to full advantage.

When he'd dazed her completely by sucking on her tongue and rasping the edges of his teeth over it, he spun her around. Coming up close behind her, he bracketed her hips with his arms and closed his hands around the ebony railing in front of them.

"Grab it, Linley," he ordered seductively in her ear.

Her hesitation earned her a swat on the exposed cheek of her ass. She jumped, partly from surprise, and partly from something darker—needier—that wormed through her psyche.

"Now."

She did as directed. An instant later, Ryder captured her hips and pulled them back. He nudged her feet outward, spreading her wide. Suddenly she was thankful for the cool, solid bar in her grip. It helped steady her when the world spun in dizzying circles.

"What are you doing?" She glanced over her shoulder,

still never abandoning the steady reference he'd given her.
"Ridding you of this lingerie." He snarled as he hooked
his fingers in the delicate straps at her hip. "It *is* beautiful,
though I'm sure I'll prefer you naked. Don't freak. I'll
replace it."

"What?" She began to blink out of the sensual haze his
undeniable authority had lulled her into.

The pressure on her hipbone built as he grasped the
pretty material and yanked. The muscles in his chest and
arms bulged an instant before the lace gave way with an
audible tear that drew the attention of a couple passing by.

"Someone's in for an evening to remember…" The man
chuckled to his partner before they disappeared into one of
the Downstairs' playrooms.

Linley shrieked. "Everyone will see."

"I know." Ryder grinned. "And every last one of the
men, plus some of the women, will know I'm the luckiest
bastard here tonight. The Basement is naked only, wildcat."

She grimaced, then shrugged.

"Good girl." He petted her bare flank, certainly enjoying
the view if the bob of his straining hard-on was any
indication. "Now face forward and don't turn around again
unless I tell you to."

He rose behind her, taking a moment to pause so that his
pelvis aligned with the crack of her ass. The weight of his
cock, which nestled between her cheeks, made her shiver.
And certainly not because she was cold.

How could she feel chilled with him pressed tight to her,
warming more than her body with his expert handling?
Adventure, risk within limits, this crazy connection they
shared, and the freedom to do what she had longed for all
mixed into a ball of need that rocketed her beyond her
inhibitions.

"Please, Ryder," she begged. "I need you to fuck me."

Rich laughter rained onto her back, which was parallel to

the floor. "I don't think so. Not yet, wildcat. You don't want me bad enough."

"I do." She nearly shouted.

"When will you realize you're not in the driver's seat anymore?" He fisted her hair around his palm and wrist, leaning in close even as he forced her head to lift. Whispering in her ear, he promised, "I'll take good care of you. On my time. In my way. If you're lucky, I'll let you choose which Basement room we wind up in. But you'd better behave if you'd like to pick."

Linley couldn't help herself. She twisted her head, testing the grip he had on her. The physical one, anyway. There was no doubt about the hold he had over her sexuality tonight. She'd follow him anywhere and obey his instructions because deep down she knew it was all designed for her pleasure.

Henry wouldn't have allowed her to participate if anything else had been the case. He'd promised her it was safe here. Ryder reassured her with butterfly kisses on her cheek.

"You're pretty when you're defiant." He spanked the other side of her ass, making her dance for him. "Does that mean you like to be punished?"

"Wouldn't know." She managed to inform him through gritted teeth.

Though honestly, she had some clue if the dampness between her thighs was any indication.

"You've never played rough before?" He gentled his clutch and his tone a tiny fraction. Enough that she rebelled.

"No. But don't you dare slack off. I'm strong enough to take you. All of you." The sting of his treatment surprised her.

"Don't worry, wildcat." He bit her shoulder. "I didn't mean to insult you. I don't doubt the stuff you're made of. Look at you. Shining on your very first night."

"Damn straight." She relaxed a bit when he gripped her tighter. With his strong embrace, she knew he'd keep her in place. The revelation was freeing.

"So let's get to it." He slid one hand up the inside of her leg from her knee to the apex of her thighs, teasing over her now-naked pussy and even her ass. Then he moved on, dragging smooth nails up her spine until they encountered the clasp of her bra.

Unhooking it with a single deft flick, he allowed her breasts to hang free.

Ryder relinquished his grip on her hair. She rested her forehead on the railing and closed her eyes to savor the skimming of his hands over her shoulder blades then around her rib cage to cradle the mounds of her chest in his palms beneath the loose cups of her bra. Her nipples had to be stabbing his hands.

Aching, hard, and aroused, she tried to rub against him.

In an instant, his hands were gone, returning only in a slap on her bare ass.

"If you can't stay still on your own, I'll help you." He growled as he wrapped an arm around her and used it to tug her upright. His hands swept along her shoulders, knocking her bra straps off them. The delicate garment fell to the floor, forgotten. "First, let me look at what's mine…tonight."

Did he hesitate because he'd like to stake a greater claim?

God, she hoped so.

Because when she faced the man before her and the intimate desire lasering from his stare, she hoped she could possess him too. One night just wasn't going to be enough. No matter how amazing it had already turned out to be.

"Hell." He stood there, fists clenched by his sides as he scanned her from head to toe.

When she reached out to him, he stumbled backward. Her hand hovered in midair.

41

"Give me a second." His breath sawed in and out of his rapidly expanding and deflating chest. "Shit. Sorry."

This time he cupped her hand in his and raised it to cover his hammering heart. The disc of his nipple tightened beneath the heel of her palm. "You're affected too?"

"You're only noticing now?" He grimaced. "I'm usually a lot better at this whole dominating stuff."

"Seem to be doing fine to me." She smiled shyly.

"I can't keep my distance with you." Ryder lifted her hand again, this time to nibble her knuckles with enough tenderness to melt her heart and any lingering flakes of frost caused by her recent introduction to a world he knew so well.

"At least we're in this together then." Linley rose onto her tiptoes to ask for a kiss. It wasn't often she had to stretch to meet a man. The extra height he had on her tall frame pleased her.

Ryder obliged. He banded her in his strong arms and plastered them together from chest to toes. His stiff cock was trapped between them as they made out as if it were a limited-time deal. Hell, maybe it was.

What would happen after tonight?

Linley swore she'd enjoy every second until they parted ways. This could be her only chance to burn so bright.

"We are," he whispered before giving her puffy lower lip one last nibble. "Now let's get that fine ass to the Basement so I can show it off. The sooner you march down those stairs, the sooner we can apply for a room. You do want my cock buried in you in the near future, don't you, wildcat?"

Grateful for his arm, which snaked around her waist, Linley nodded. She adored how easily he turned her knees to jelly. Everything in her strained to get closer to him. "Yes, sir."

"You have no idea what it does to me when you call me that." Ryder growled.

"I think I have a clue." She glanced at the erection he sported. Thick, dark, and damp at the tip, there was no mistaking his arousal.

"Probably true." The genuine amusement in his laugh hit her again. His similar sense of humor turned her on more than his not-quite-perfect good looks. The man ticked all her boxes and then some. "Careful. The treads are windy and it gets darker. Let your eyes adjust. I've got you."

He ushered her down the spiral staircase into the Basement.

"Oh, wow." She gasped as the night became a little more interesting, if such a thing was possible. Midnight paint graced ornate wood. Red accents became the highlight. Instead of seeming creepy, the ambiance lent itself to tucking closer to Ryder.

He braced her as they leveled out onto the dark boards of the flooring, covered in area rugs plush enough to curl her toes in. Instead of the refined sexuality of the area above, the Basement didn't seek to sugarcoat anything. Leather seats directly faced black-painted equipment on a stone wall that would have put a medieval dungeon to shame.

Cries of torture were absent. But those of pure delight ran rampant.

Transfixed, she watched a woman writhe on a giant X leaned against the wall. Two men alternated delivering light blows with a tool sporting wide strips of some soft-looking material. "What's that?"

Ryder stroked her hair. Patiently he explained, "The men are flogging her. It's an introductory lesson. The Master on the right has been training her husband. Eventually he'll graduate to a more intense implement."

"That looks pretty extreme to me." She wondered why it also turned her on. Moisture began to spill from her pussy onto the tops of her thighs, making her slightly self-conscious. Could Ryder tell?

From his flared nostrils when he glanced down at her, she guessed he could.

"Don't tell me you dislike the idea. Does it look as if she's enjoying herself?" Ryder gripped her chin and refused to allow her to glance away from the pure delight on the woman's face as she stared longingly at her husband and the man he was willing to learn how to delight her from.

"Hell yes." She sputtered.

"All right then." Ryder nudged her forward with his knuckles between her shoulder blades. "Now wait until they watch you take your first spanking. You're going to distract them all with your sweet submission. You're a natural, Linley."

She balked. In a lame attempt to delay, she objected. "Aren't you going to show me the rooms first? My options?"

"You've trusted fate—and me—an awful lot tonight." Ryder teased her earlobe with his teeth as he coaxed her into making a crazy decision, one she craved but would never have had the guts to opt for. "Why not see it through? I can't wait much longer to have you. Let's take the next available. We'll make it ours, whatever we're dealt. Remember, I won't let you fall."

Without debating, she zeroed in on the tone of his voice and the protective hold he had on her. She believed. When a server wearing a crisscross of black leather, and nothing else, passed nearby, she called out, "Excuse me. I'd like to put us on the waiting list."

The man paused. Though subtle in his expression, his appreciation couldn't be missed or faked as his cock hardened before her eyes. "Master Ryder has a new toy? This should be fun."

"Less commentary. More tendering of the lady's request." Ryder spoke in a firm tone the man responded to instantly.

"Yes sir." He bowed and spun away.

"Thank you, Jay." Ryder made sure to soften the point of his impatience.

"You're welcome." The man smiled over his shoulder. "I'm glad my break is due in a minute. A woman who riles you. This I *have* to see."

Linley raised a brow as she met Ryder's stare.

He shrugged. "There's no use denying it. I've been pretty frank about your impact on me, haven't I, wildcat?"

"It's nice to know it's not only me in a whole new world." She nibbled her bottom lip, loving the dilation of his pupils.

"Something special is happening tonight." He kissed her hard, then scooped her into his arms. "I plan to take full advantage."

Ryder strode to the corner of the Basement. He plunked her down on her knees on two miniature platforms, which perched on top of black stilts. One supported each of her legs from mid-shin to knee. Her feet dangled off the ends. A little confused, she waited for Ryder to bend her over a rounded support, also elevated, at waist level. Next he placed each of her hands through a leather tube farther forward. At the end of each, a handle made a convenient place for her to grip and balance the weight of her upper body.

Though she never would have believed it, the minimalist contraption was actually quite comfortable, even after Ryder yanked on a cord that constricted the tubes around her arms, trapping her effectively.

Momentary panic had her testing the bonds. They were immovable.

"Shh." Ryder was beside her in an instant. "It's a natural response. Animal instinct. Use your mind, wildcat. Trust your body. You want this."

One hand rubbed her back as the other slipped between her legs. Given the fluid glide of his fingers, she couldn't deny the arousal coating her thicker by the instant.

She slowed her breathing and allowed herself to consider the reassuring pressure on her wrists and forearms.

"There you go." Ryder kissed her cheek before wandering toward her feet. "Now you've got it. Here come two more. For your safety, Linley. Wouldn't want you to fall. You've already proved staying still is a challenge. And I'm going to spank you harder than I did earlier. Where all my friends can see your ass turning pink for me."

"Will it hurt?" She swallowed hard, gripping the handles fractionally tighter.

"Only a bit. I'll rub it and kiss it better." Something pinched her ass. If she wasn't mistaken, he might have taken a bite. "I need a distraction until our room is ready. You'd better hope it's not long."

She moaned at his bantering.

As if the cry unchained something in him, his palm met her bottom with a slap that sounded a hell of a lot worse than it felt. Still she yelped. Surprised. And ruthlessly excited.

"Oh, come on. Wildcat, you can take more than that." He chuckled at her response. Still, he soothed the sting as he'd promised, with gentle circles from his fingers. They wandered from her ass, between her legs. His simple reward had her begging for more.

"That's better." He obliged her with three or four more smacks.

She lost track around the time she realized there was a display on the wall in front of her, not four feet away, that noted the names of the rooms and their statuses.

"Ah, found the scoreboard, did you?" Ryder talked low and steady as he massaged the tingles from her ass. Except as she read she only found herself wanting more of his blunt contact.

Whips and Chains. Fuck Machines Rule. Wax Museum. Pins and Needles. More the Merrier. She's The Boss. The list went on, but her eyes had glazed over by the time she got that far.

Ryder made a circuit of her splayed and pinned body, taking his time and touching every exposed surface. She praised his foresight when she couldn't stay put. Had she not been strapped down, she would have busted her ass very ungracefully in front of the men and women who had gathered nearby to observe him putting her through her paces.

"That's right, Linley," he cooed in her ear before kissing her with a tenderness at odds—or was it?—with the rougher treatment he lavished on her. "I know what you need. I'm going to give it to you."

This time when he came even with her ass, which was raised high in the air, he delivered a barrage of spanks that had her first crying out, then groaning, and finally moaning, attempting to rub herself on the contraption cradling her. The burn had percolated into her skin. She absorbed it as it morphed from mild discomfort to something so much more potent.

"Ryder." She called for him and he came, though he continued the constant contact of his stroking hands.

"Yes, wildcat?" She caught sight of his hard-on in her peripheral vision and knew he suffered as much as she did.

"I need you." If that meant they fucked for the first time in front of the spectators murmuring their praise, fine.

"Right here? Right now?" Ryder paced toward her feet. Would he step between her legs and slide his cock deep?

Staring straight ahead, waiting for the pressure his blunt cap would put on the entrance to her pussy, she noticed immediately when the switchboard lights flipped. She blinked, focusing on the vacancy directory on the wall in front of her to determine their destiny.

Except there wasn't one new green light.

There were two.

"Ryder!" She didn't care that her shout was less than

dignified.

He must have caught her urgency because he bent over her in a flash. "That was a close one, wildcat. Lucky again. So what do we have here?"

He hummed as her gaze flickered wildly between the options. Both were delicious, but one held more appeal to her at the moment. Would Ryder feel the same? What would he select?

"It's your night, Linley. And you've been such a good girl for me." He continued to rub the sting from her prominently displayed ass. Other men in the crowd supplied their assent with his obvious intentions. "Which will it be? Fuck Machines Rule or More the Merrier?"

If Linley picked *Fuck Machines Rule,* turn to page 27, *Fuck Machines Rule.*

If Linley picked *More the Merrier,* turn to page 49, *More The Merrier.*

More The Merrier

"I'd love to try More the Merrier. If you're up for it,"
Linley amended.

A rush of murmurs went through the crowd. Several men
volunteered as quickly as if they'd been on the *Family Feud*
faceoff, their hands hovering over the buzzer.

The admission to Ryder—never mind publicly declaring
her debauchery—would have mortified her earlier in the
evening. Any discomfort she'd felt about sharing her desires
seemed to have vanished somewhere around the time she'd
begged her usher to fuck her out in the open for everyone to
witness.

About then she'd realized she was proud of her passion
and the man who managed to magnify its impact on her. Here
among others who understood the need for something more
than the everyday dating drama—something lustier,
something more direct, something darker—for whatever their
personal reasons, Linley could be honest.

Ryder had unlocked that capability in her. A huge win.
She embraced the change.

Her escort singled out a couple of the men who'd been
watching her closely.

"Grant, help me get her loose and you can join us. Todd,
I'm going to need you too. You're both available tonight,
correct?" Her seemingly easygoing guide flashed his inner
core of steel. Authority sat naturally on him, even if he chose
not to don the mantle most of the time. What did he do to
earn that? Where did it come from in real life?

A tendril of recognition stirred within her. Part of her
related on a level that insisted he hid a heck of a lot behind
his jeans and T-shirt exterior. Or maybe that was her

justification for the fairly major omissions she'd had to make to follow the rules.

In any case, she didn't have long to dwell on the possibilities as Ryder's two recruits freed her in no time flat. Having three strong men surrounding her tilted her world on its axis. Funny enough, she had no trouble telling which person was Ryder. Already they'd formed a bond.

Linley felt off balance, both because of her line of reasoning and because the comfort of her bindings had been stripped away. She tumbled right into Ryder's outstretched arms. He winked down at her as he cradled her against his toasty chest. "Hey there."

"Hi," she whispered with a smile, growing meek just for a moment. It was either that or admit how much more than simply her body was in the game tonight. Unwise, she'd come to care during the evening they'd shared.

The Basement shifted around her as Ryder toted her to the appropriate portal. She didn't notice much of the surroundings since her stare never wavered from his scruffy jaw. The deep, rich brown of his hair made her long to run her fingers through it and the matching trail that lead down his body to his cock.

All along the way, men and women alike congratulated the two men now flanking Ryder and her as they made their way to a private chamber. Some people cursed them or joked about volunteering to pinch hit.

Ryder brushed them aside, taking his dream team into the shadows near the row of rooms. He stepped aside, using his allies as an extension of himself. Grant depressed the latch-style handle. He held the door for Ryder.

When he slipped inside, he didn't immediately turn on the lights.

"I'm glad you decided on this room, wildcat." Under cover of darkness, he confessed, "I don't mind sharing. Giving my playmate that extra level of pleasure is an honor.

And later, I'll stake my claim on you privately. I'm not going to lie. Something about you has me possessive."

"You sure you want us to stay, Ryder?" Smooth and sexy, Todd's low key question put her a little more at ease. She didn't know these men. But Ryder did. And if he trusted them, that was good enough for her.

"We can go out the side door so no one sees if you're worried about appearances," Grant offered.

Ryder looked to her and her alone. "It's your call, wildcat. I'm up for whatever you desire."

"I didn't come this far to back out now. Let's do it." She smiled over his shoulder at his friends and tossed them a timid finger wave.

They were good-looking guys, that's for sure. Grant had a suave air about him. All his motions were fluid and graceful. Though he wasn't as tall or as broad as Ryder, he had a lean, lithe body that tempted her to touch. And that was even before her gaze wandered over his long erection. "Hello to you too, sweetheart. Ryder sure did hit the newbie jackpot tonight."

Todd grinned. "And us too."

Linley switched her focus to the rough-and-tumble man. His enormous shoulders and powerful thighs made her fairly sure he had to be a professional athlete, or a trainer, or a body builder. His blond hair and rich green eyes helped keep him from looking too sinister. Despite his size, he was gentle when he stroked her hair. "You're very pretty, Linley. And brave to wander down here your first time out."

"Hell, it took Todd two years at Underground before he made it to the Basement." Grant poked fun at his friend.

When they looked as though they might deteriorate into roughhousing, which Grant stood no chance at winning in brute strength—though maybe in swiftness or agility—Ryder took charge.

"Focus guys, or I'll find a new set of sidekicks. I'm not

messing around with Linley's experience. Tonight should be special for her. Perfect." He leaned down and kissed her lightly. "I want her to remember this for the rest of her life."

"Pretty sure you've already achieved that goal." She turned her cheek into his palm when he cupped her face.

"When did you become such a bleeding-heart romantic?" Todd wiggled his eyebrows at Ryder. Grant had the good sense to step in.

"Don't worry about me. Concentrate on bringing your *A* game." Ryder threw Linley over his shoulder, as if to prove he still had his swagger. She didn't mind. It got her to the bed that much faster. She laughed as she bounced when he tossed her into the center then climbed on.

Ryder sat beside her, propping her up on no less than thirty silk-cased pillows. He held her hand as he curled his fingers toward his outstretched palm, inviting his friends to join them. "Todd, you can make up for that smart mouth by getting over here and putting it to better use."

The bed dipped as the two large men added their weight to the mattress. They stalked closer to her. Their heated stares on her splayed, naked body had her shivering in Ryder's protective hold. "Nothing to worry about, wildcat. They're actually decent lovers. Not as good as me, but…close enough."

Grant shared a conspiratorial grin with Todd. "That sounded like a challenge."

"It sure did." He crawled toward her like a predator on the prowl. Ryder and Grant did the friendly thing and each wrapped a broad hand around one of her knees. They spread her wide for their buddy.

Linley squeaked, then turned her face into Ryder's chest.

He was quick to correct her. "No. Don't hide from what they make you feel. It's okay to enjoy what they give you. Remember, it's all a gift from me to you. Think of them like my extra sets of hands. Or tongues."

Grant cracked his civilized veneer when he snorted. Todd took his cue. He dove between her legs, parting her thighs and spreading them wider to accommodate his bulk. The first swipe of his hot mouth over her mound had her arching off the bed. The other two men ensured she stayed in place for their friend. Ryder claimed her mouth and reached across her chest, pinning her to the mattress while Grant secured her leg and petted her belly. The overwhelming presence of the three men incited a riot of mini-tremors in the general region of her womb.

Todd paused his oral explorations long enough to lift his head and say, "Damn, she's delicious. And I can feel the little kisses of her pussy as it flexes. She's already so wet. Can I put my fingers in her, Ry?"

"Don't let me stop you." He laughed. "Just go slow. Your hands are as fucking thick as the rest of you."

Linley moaned as she considered what those proportions meant for his cock. She couldn't wait to find out. And somehow it didn't feel like a free for all with three men. It still seemed like one extreme encounter with the single guy who'd elected to show her this good time.

Grant didn't have to be told. He focused his attention on Linley's left breast, suckling and plumping the flesh until she was distracted enough for Todd to introduce his fingers into her pussy. Ryder alternated between soothing her with gentle reassurance and mimicking Grant's caresses on her other breast.

Six hands caressed her inside and out. The intensity of their attention overwhelmed her with desire. She reached out and tucked her fingers in Ryder's hair. Softness feathered between them, calming her and grounding her during the storm of passion that whipped around her.

Todd groaned from between her legs. She watched as his ass clenched. He humped the silk sheets, rubbing himself on the bed while he feasted on her. The taste of her, or maybe the feel of her smothering his fat finger, certainly turned him on.

Suddenly Linley went from feeling shy for indulging in such decadence, to embracing the empowerment they gave her. They made her feel desirable beyond belief. A goddess to be worshipped.

The thought alone had her pussy clamping hard on Todd's intruding digit.

"Damn," his reverent mumble served to vibrate her engorged clit, which he now flicked his tongue across. Ryder was right. The big man was a good lover. Her body responded, and she poured her ecstasy into a deep kiss with her escort.

When they broke apart, both of them panting, he grinned. "You really like that, huh?"

"Mmm." She hung on to both Grant and Ryder, trying to ground herself.

"Damn," Grant trailed his fingers up and down her body. "She's gorgeous. More and more by the minute. Is she going to come soon, Todd?"

"I can make her tip over any time you like." The smug grin he flashed when he paused his skilled eating made her tummy flip.

She wished she could deny it. That she had more willpower than that. But Ryder took one look into her lust-glazed eyes and knew Todd wasn't boasting for nothing.

"Do it." Ryder commanded his friend. "Set her off."

He left Todd to work his magic and instead focused on her. The impact of his attention increased her enjoyment exponentially. "Let go Linley."

She did as he ordered.

Her body and heart responded without giving her brain a chance to opt out. While she shuddered, soaking in the bliss racing through her veins, the three men around her held her, soothed her, enhanced her euphoria until she could hardly catch her breath.

Todd's finger was forced from her body by the spasms of her pussy.

"Let me taste her." Grant groaned, rubbing his hard-on against her hip.

Todd nodded. She expected the men to switch places, but instead Todd held out his hand and Grant suckled his extended fingers, cleaning them in a matter of seconds. Their unabashed sharing had her pussy spilling more juice by the second.

"Damn," Grant mumbled when his mouth was empty once more. In their deliciously direct way, he said, "I'm dying here. Let me fuck her, Ry? Unless you want the first shot?"

Linley appreciated his lack of game playing and veiled innuendo.

"No. I don't care who has her before me. I want to be the *last* person she takes. Tonight…" He trailed off as if he intended to say more.

Todd cleared his throat, saving Ryder from the awkward pause. He breathed heavily as he switched places with Grant then caressed her breasts. "Your girl's got a damn near perfect rack. You know how I love to fuck a nice pair of tits."

"Would you let him, Linley?" Ryder smiled indulgently at them.

"Yes." She tried not to shout and managed, sort of.

"Good girl." Ryder got to his knees beside her head. "And how about me? Suck me while they ride you? For their pleasure and yours. Just not too much. I'm not coming until I'm buried inside you. Okay?"

Verbal assurance was not possible because she'd leaned forward and engulfed his cock before he'd even finished talking.

The tearing of a foil pouch sounded through the grunts

of the three men, who satisfied themselves and her in the process. An instant later, Grant invaded her still quivering pussy. Linley gasped, which only served to allow Ryder deeper in her mouth. The blunt head of his cock nudged her throat, painting the taste of his pre-come on the back of her tongue.

And just when she thought she couldn't take anymore, Todd straddled her easily. He gathered her breasts, smooshing them together around the length of his cock, which landed in the valley between them with a distinct *thud* on her breastbone.

"You're amazing, wildcat." Ryder stroked her hair and traced her stretched lips around his cock. "Taking three of us isn't easy. Not for some women. You're a natural. So generous."

Linley thanked him for his praise by swirling her tongue along the underside of his shaft. His thighs corded beside her and he froze.

"Not too much of that." He tapped her chin. "I won't last if you do more. How's it going over there Grant?"

The gentleman lost most of his chivalry as he plowed into her deeper and faster with every stroke. Though there were lots of distractions, his efforts became harder to ignore as her channel began the pattern of tightening all over again.

"She's strangling me." He grunted. "We can make her come again. Soon."

Todd gurgled as he slipped and slid between the globes of her breasts. He pinched her nipples, twisting just enough to add to her rapture. "I'm probably not going to be able to hold off if I watch this pretty face coming. Especially while she's going to town on Ryder like he's some kind of candy."

Grant groaned. "You're making her hotter when you talk like that. Shit, I don't think I can make it. I'm going to come. Any second."

The urgency of his play by play did Linley in. She stared

up into Ryder's eyes. He smiled and nodded. Soaring again, she wrung every last drop of Grant's restraint from him along with his seed. He poured blast after blast of come into the condom he wore.

True to his word, Todd observed her surrender and joined her. He painted her chest with searing streaks of pearlescent fluid. To see a man as big and strong as him reduced by the utter devastation of his inhibitions spiraled her climax higher. She continued to wring Grant's embedded hard-on until he softened and pulled out.

Still her body demanded more. Unsatisfied, she needed the one man she hadn't yet pleased.

Todd rolled to his back, puffing on the mattress beside her. He collected himself as Grant leaned forward and kissed her cheek beside Ryder's twitching cock, which still spread her jaw almost uncomfortably wide. "You were magnificent."

Grant's kisses trailed down her cheek and neck until he could massage the proof of Todd's release into her skin. She gleamed with another man's come, but it only seemed to make Ryder want her more. He retreated from her mouth and caught the condom Todd tossed him in midair.

"Would you guys mind if we finished this alone?" He clapped Grant on the shoulder then bumped fists with Todd. "Thanks."

"Anytime," they replied in unison.

"Welcome to Underground, Linley." Grant squeezed her hand then abandoned the bed. Todd followed suit. She didn't know or care where they went after that because Ryder claimed his rightful spot between her legs.

She wrapped him in her arms and welcomed him within her, against her body. He blanketed her, uncaring about the way his chest slid against hers in the remnants of Todd's orgasm. He advanced inside her, using her copious arousal and the pre-stretched tissue to his best advantage.

Instead of the fast and furious pounding she expected from the man who'd been on edge for a while, his tender glides within her brought tears to her eyes.

"At the end of the day, this is all I need," he whispered to her. "This connection between us guarantees the sex will be stellar even without all the bells and whistles."

He validated the truth of his statement by showing her over and over.

When he pressed inside to the hilt then retreated, sometimes taking his cock all the way out so they could enjoy his reentry again and again, she shivered all over. The intensity of his stare, and the butterfly kisses he dusted over her lips, had her poised on the verge of another climax when she would have thought it impossible.

Linley ran her hands up and down the flexing muscles of Ryder's back. She grabbed his ass and held him deep within her. Staring into each other's eyes, motionless except for the press and release of their pelvises grinding on each other, they unraveled.

Ryder shouted her name. He bent down and bit her neck, sucking ferociously, the pressure at odds with his gentle rocks within her body. Contrasting sensations and the joy flooding her soul had her coming with him.

Her body hugged him tight as they enjoyed each other.

The ground-shaking orgasm went on—long and low— for what seemed like forever.

When it faded to occasional aftershocks, they collapsed together.

To find out what happened next, turn to page 147, *Ryder Epilogue.*

Linley Picked Chase

"You won't regret that decision, love." The dazzling white smile Chase shared with her sent a thrill racing through her belly. He entwined their fingers and squeezed.

"You might not, but if you do…you know where to find me." Ryder kissed her cheek, impressing the faint scratch of his stubble on her lips before sliding from the table with the grace of a jungle cat.

"Nice seeing you again." The sportsmanlike clap he landed on Chase's shoulder enhanced her regard for the men and this place that had culled would-be sleaze balls from their roster with extreme prejudice.

"Better luck next time."

"Enjoy." Ryder saluted them both before wandering over to a group of women who damn near swooned as he focused the intensity of his attention on them. The view of his jeans-clad ass was pretty damn spectacular.

"Buyer's remorse?" Chase flashed his dimples and the gorgeous crinkles around his eyes, which proclaimed his naturally happy disposition.

"Not at all." She chuckled. He put her at ease effortlessly.

"Then here's to the best night of our lives." He lifted his flute and clinked it against hers.

"Those are high expectations." Linley raised her brows. "You do realize I have no idea what the hell I'm doing, right?"

"Used to taking charge and leading the way, huh?" His insightfulness attracted her as much as his gorgeous face.

"You could say that. Yes." She tried not to scoff at the understatement of the century.

The sound of his laughter did funny things to her insides. "Sweetheart, you're here. I'm here. And I'm already sure this is not an ordinary evening for either of us."

"But…you've done this before, right?" Was she violating the rules by asking?

"I've been around." He reassured her. "But never with a woman like you. There's something between us, Linley. Don't you feel it too?"

"I picked you didn't I?" She found herself edging closer to him, wondering how his solid chest would feel beneath her fingers. The urge to knead his pecs like a kitten built in her. Something about him made her want to lean on him as she hadn't done with a man…probably ever.

"Yes." When he tilted his head, a lock of sun-bronzed hair fell over his forehead. Not knowing what he did for a living both intrigued and frustrated her. With that sleek yet defined build and the streaks in his hair, she might have pegged him for a construction worker.

His Armani suit and fancy talk said otherwise.

"Linley?" There went that smile again, lighting him up a fraction of an inch at a time.

"Sorry, what?" She blinked from her daze.

"I asked why you chose me."

"Oh." Her pause allowed her to gather her thoughts. "I guess because you made me feel comfortable even though I'm not sure yet what I'm looking for, and I thought you offered a bigger range of options, instead of only the hardcore stuff. Including possibly choosing nothing at all."

"Does that mean you're considering bailing?"

"Well…" Would she piss him off if she admitted her uncertainty in the face of this place? She hadn't expected it to be so complex. So enthralling. Or addictive. Diverse and vast. In her mind, Underground had resembled a seedy bar with loud music and quick, dirty fun in a shadowed backroom.

This was…personal.

"How about we take a look around? Who knows, you might see something you'd like to try. We could get another drink and dance a little before you decide." The jiggle he gave the empty bottle of champagne surprised her. Where had it all gone?

Her dry glass proved she'd gulped her share twice over. Maybe that accounted for her blissful lightheadedness. Doubtful. Chase affected her more than the alcohol. Hints of his scent—vanilla, sandalwood, and pure man—entranced her. Instant attraction coursed through her veins. She could only imagine what it would be like to have him in her arms while they swayed to music she could hear faintly as it drifted from somewhere out of sight. Or have him over her in a soft bed.

Well, maybe she wouldn't have to rely on fantasies for long.

All she had to do was take his hand.

She did.

Linley blushed when he helped her stand, righting the dress Ryder had set askew. If his hands lingered over the curve of her ass, she didn't object. He tucked her close and cupped her elbow as he led her away from the dark-haired man, who glanced at them over his shoulder despite the harem of willing ladies who lounged at his feet while he commanded a large armchair by the fire.

"I suppose we don't have to feel too bad for our friend," Chase snickered.

"And you wouldn't prefer to be the center of all that attention tonight?" She didn't attempt to rein in her curiosity.

"Ever hear the saying quality versus quantity?" He trailed his fingers up her wrist then to her shoulder. Every sweep of his hand brushed exposed skin. "I relish the finer things in life. And you're clearly one of those, Linley."

Both men had been willing to entertain her. Hell, they'd

practically fought for the privilege. That alone went a long
way toward boosting her confidence. Out of her comfort
zone, she allowed Chase to have control.

Was that what she'd been missing on all those almost-
great dates? Ones where she'd dictated the time, the
place...the *everything*? If nothing else, tonight promised her
insights she'd blinded herself to for months.

The hallway opened into a ballroom. She gasped as she
took in the naughty fairy-tale surroundings. It seemed almost
like a masquerade ball as people in a wide spectrum of dress,
from jeans to leather to fancy gowns to nothing at all,
circulated in the space.

Black and white marble checked the floor. Mirrors
reflected revelry from every angle. Bold splashes of jewel-
toned furniture littered the area. She sort of expected to see
the Queen of Hearts stride by, except this time she'd be
decked head to toe in a red and white harlequin latex cat suit.

"Thirsty?" Chase paused at an opulent bar.

Linley swallowed twice but couldn't force out a
response, so she nodded instead.

"Will a Château Margaux Bordeaux do?" He beamed
when she narrowed her eyes.

Just how much had Henry blabbed to Underground
about her in the fifteen minutes he'd had to arrange this
escapade? Enough that Chase and Ryder had been equipped
with her name as well as her favorite wine.

What else did her date know?

Chase raised his hand when he caught the bartender's
eye. He flashed some sort of hand signal then motioned to a
settee along one wall. His heat returned to her arm and they
continued the short journey, sinking together into the
deceptively comfortable couch.

Perfecting her poker face had been important early on
when she was young. Competitors or associates had believed
they could take advantage of her. Tonight, she wasn't sure

she managed to employ the tool to its full advantage.
It might have helped if she hadn't stared at the
menagerie before her.

"It's nice to see this place through your eyes, Linley."
Chase draped an arm around her shoulder, drawing her to his
chest. She gladly snuggled up to the shelter he provided
while she continued to scan the crowd of liberated pleasure
seekers.

This is what she'd been missing. Here she could cut
straight to the heart of the matter without bogging herself
down in the politics of a boyfriend or the image she had to
uphold.

"How so?" She finally found her voice. Could she give
something back to the man promising to erase her failures
and replace them with something steamy? Something life-
altering. A no-strings release.

"Maybe I've become jaded." He sighed, accepting her
caress on his shoulder and onto the plane of his chest.
Touching him was a decadent indulgence. Granting him
some solace was a bonus. "I sometimes forget about these
simple pleasures in my haste to enjoy…the rest."

"What else is there?" She didn't realize she nibbled on
her bottom lip until he pried it from between her teeth with
the pad of his thumb, soothing the sting.

"Ah." From a gorgeous server in skin-tight lace, Chase
accepted his drink. Expensive whiskey, if the rich amber tone
and hint of oak was any indication. She did the same with her
glass of wine, grateful to have something to wet her throat
with. "Well, you've seen most of the ground floor. The
dining area and the fireside lounge plus the ballroom. There's
also a library with a piano I'd love to play for you sometime.
And a game room, the vanilla variety—pool, darts, cards. All
ways for people to meet someone they might like to sink
down a level or two with."

She nodded, laying her head on his shoulder between

sips of her wine. He didn't discourage her affection, so she went one step farther, resting her hand on his thigh. Damn he was hard all over. And hot. Her fingers explored the seam of his tailored slacks.

After letting her roam, he began to reciprocate. First by stroking her hair, running his fingers through the mussed tresses. Then he drew swirls along her spine, humming as he reached the swell of her ass.

"What happens once there's a connection?" The huskiness of her murmur surprised her.

"Then it's time to go farther underground. The entrance to Downstairs is at the other end of this room. See the gold railing over there?" He gestured with his tumbler.

When she followed the line, she noticed an ornate balustrade at the top of a wide marble staircase. Every once in a while, a couple—or more—would drift down it and disappear. Less frequently, probably since the night was young, someone would emerge. Their sleepy, satisfied smiles told her all she needed to know.

"Most people refer to it as *stooping to your level.*" He chuckled.

"That's terrible." She buried her face in the crook of his neck for an instant. Long enough to breathe deep, getting drunk on him.

"Much more of that and we'll be breaking the no-sex-on-the-Underground-floor rule." Chase swiped her empty glass from her hand. He set it, along with his, on a side table then asked her to dance.

The music seemed to change from song to song, the mix as eclectic as the gathering gyrating to its beat. She knew this one. The Wanted's "Glad You Came" seemed appropriate.

"So are you?" Chase stared into her eyes as he tucked her to his chest and began to rock. During the faster sections, the graceful swing of his hips advertised just how much rhythm he had, and that he knew how to put his body to good use.

"Hmm?" She blinked, starting to lose herself in the place, the moment, and the man.

"Happy to be here?" Before permitting her to respond, he stacked the deck way in his favor by leaning closer and pressing his mouth to hers. His kiss was like him—intense yet subtle. Sophisticated. Delicious.

Invigorating.

For the first time since she'd bought Lane Technology's largest competitor almost a year ago, she felt truly alive. Adrenaline rushed through her system as he seduced her lips with his. And still they swayed to the more sedate section of the hit. The brush of his tongue had her sighing. He took advantage of the opportunity to insinuate himself more completely.

If the smell of him had been nice, the taste of him...

Linley rose onto her tiptoes. It was rare for her to meet a man tall enough to require the gesture. He made her feel feminine as she sealed them together more completely. She devoured him as if she hadn't had an amazing meal less than two hours ago. The flavor of desire satisfied her far more than the decadent chocolate dessert she'd enjoyed at L'Etoile.

"I'll take that as a yes," he whispered against her lips when he ended the exchange. "Me too, by the way."

Lost in their renewed dance, she didn't notice he'd edged her toward the rear of the ballroom until the path Downstairs appeared near her feet. The crowd sang the refrain. While they did, Chase stepped onto the first wide tread. He crooked his fingers and waited for her to join him.

"I..." She hesitated. "I'm not sure."

"Come take a peek. We won't go in just yet. There's a lounge of sorts at the bottom. Sometimes people wait for a prearranged partner or take a break there. Plus, it's where the restrooms are. Refreshments are available for those who are playing especially hard, to get their energy back. We can talk more, away from the music." He didn't grab for her. Instead, he waited. Patient. Understanding.

Linley swallowed hard.

"Give it a few minutes. If you're uncomfortable, we'll leave." His soft smile encouraged her. "No pressure, love."

"If you're not a salesman, you're missing out on a big opportunity." She shook her head although she grinned. The heel of her shoe clicked on the stone when she joined him.

"I've been told I can be…persuasive." His fingers curled around her arm, keeping her balanced as they descended together. "Go slow. Look at the murals."

She sighed, doing as he suggested. The beautiful artwork reminded her of a sordid version of a historic opera house. Cherubs hovered over couples, blessing them with all sorts of naughty inspiration. Exotic, beautiful people—too proportional to have been painted from imagination—entangled themselves in amorous embraces of all sorts.

"See how those two are watching the couple by the stream?" Chase pointed out a particular section of the painting.

"Yes." She followed the direction of his long finger.

"It's not just a pretty thing, Linley." He paused, tipping her face toward his and stealing another brief kiss. "Think of it sort of like a menu."

"Oh!" She leaned forward, her head swiveling at the variety of delights.

"So many things to choose from?" She didn't mean to gasp out loud.

"Only limited by your imagination really." He spread his hands out. "A little farther and you can see one of my favorites."

"Show me." Curious about his desires, she followed him to a landing in the middle of the run of stairs.

"This part." He angled his chin toward a vignette

highlighted by a halogen spotlight. The artist had paid a lot of attention to detail in this section of the lascivious landscape. Clearly it had been a passion of his or hers as well.

A pale woman stretched out on a bed of wildflowers, her hair cascading behind her like a waterfall of silk. Vines wrapped around her wrists and ankles. They held her snug to the lush meadow, open for her lover, who crawled between her legs. An impressive erection made it clear he'd enjoy the feast laid out before him.

"Does it look good to you, Linley?" When had he come so close behind her?

Chase's breath washed over the curve of her neck. His hands wrapped around her waist. No matter how hard she tried, she couldn't help but squirm in his hold.

"I wouldn't turn it down." The catch in her sassy retort highlighted her false ennui.

The clear ring of his laugh echoed off the vaulted ceiling of the way Downstairs. "Of course not. I've spent a hell of a lot of time practicing my technique. I promise satisfaction is guaranteed. Both of ours."

As they proceeded, scenes flashed before her eyes. Delights she'd never imagined along with some she'd dreamed of plenty. Sex in every position imaginable. Play with toys. Sex as a spectator sport. Even a sketch of a woman taking her partner in her ass.

"Not that." She pointed. "Not tonight. Or maybe ever."

"Your call, love." Chase kissed her cheek. "I could make you like it, but I respect your boundaries."

The closer they came to the curtain looming before them, the more daring the depictions got. Several made her uncomfortable. For sure, she was a lightweight. At least to start. What would the Basement have been like?

Too much for her. She was sure she'd made the right choice.

Maybe that's what Henry had meant earlier. *Just...pick*

your pleasures wisely, he'd cautioned.

With Chase studying her while she deliberated, she knew the time had come to decide again. What did she want this night to be like?

"You know, I meant what I said earlier." Her date paused, becoming serious. The chivalrous side of him turned her on even more than some of the drawings. "I'm not the kind of man who insists on limiting my relationships to the confines of the club. It's just that this environment is more expedient most of the time. Real life circumstances can make it difficult to find what you need on the outside. Skipping this is still an option. If you'd prefer something more traditional—private—I'd be glad to escort you home. I hope you'll invite me in, but you don't even have to go that far. If you're not ready, we can try this some other time. I can already tell you're worth waiting for, love."

Linley couldn't stop her gaze from ping-ponging between Chase's sincere smile and the fragments of silhouettes that peeped from between the crack in the rich velvet curtain before her. Soft moans and deep male grunts of pleasure drifted from the other side of the barrier.

It might as well have been a different world from the one she'd lived in her whole life.

Was that good? Or bad?

"Which would you prefer, Linley?" Chase tucked an errant curl behind her ear. "Do you want to stay here? Or shall I take you home?"

If Linley said *Home,* turn to page 102, *Happiest At Home.*

If Linley said *Downstairs,* turn to page 113, *Stay Downstairs.*

A Pinch Of Spice

"That combo is one of my specialties, love." Chase smirked. He tugged the knot of his tie, loosening it until he could slip the silk free. He dragged the end of the material across the tops of her breasts, teasing and tempting her all at the same time.

She wriggled a little beneath both the barest brush of softness and the intensity of his regard. "How about hurrying? Is that one of your strengths?"

He laughed as she'd intended. "Not so much. I like to savor my pleasures."

"Damn it." She giggled. The sense of humor they shared acted as insulation against the intensity they also generated.

"Let's get that dress off you." He lifted the hem an inch or two. "How's that for a start?"

"The right direction." Linley would have torn it off in a second flat if he'd allowed it. Instead he held her down with a palm on her sternum. The sides of her breasts hugged his hand.

"I've got this." He kissed her, but didn't linger. They both knew they'd fall into endless explorations if he let them. While part of her wouldn't have objected to an epic make-out session, the majority of her mind and body called out for more.

She planted her feet on the mattress and lifted her ass, unconcerned about the peep show she gave him between her spread thighs.

"So pretty." He caressed the inside of her knee up her leg. "I can see the lace of your panties from here."

"Hurry. You can probably admire the details better when they're flung on the floor. If you really care to." She grinned.

He made it easy to ask for what she wanted without artifice or social pleasantries.

"Pass. The best part is catching a glimpse in the shadows and knowing soon I'll be beneath them." He teased higher on her leg, his lips following the path of his hand. "I can smell you from here."

A whimper escaped when he burrowed along the edge of her hem.

"Okay," he chuckled. "I'm speeding it up. But next time, after you're more relaxed, we're going to take this slow. Really, really slow."

"Deal." The effort to pronounce that single word with her brain addled felt tougher than delivering an entire press release when she uttered it. "Get busy."

"Bossy, huh?" He fisted his fingers in the dress and yanked. The material easily rose above her breasts. It gathered there, ringing her torso just below her collarbones. Completely on display, she constricted in on herself a bit.

A man as handsome and charming as him had to have been with oodles of beautiful women. How would she stack up? It'd been a long damn time since she had reason to doubt herself. She shouldn't have bothered this time.

"Hell." Chase laid reverent strokes along her mostly flat stomach. "You're flawless. I'm glad you're new to Underground. Selfish but…I like having you to myself."

"Same goes." She smiled up at him. "At least for tonight, you're mine."

His smile pressed to hers before he began to manipulate her lips and tongue with his. Meanwhile his hands roamed over her bare skin, making her wish she could do the same to him. The firmness of his muscles beneath his clothes tempted her to start ripping and worry about his buttons later. Much later.

Linley didn't have to hope for long.

They broke apart, both struggling to draw in a deep

breath.

When Chase separated them, he finished stripping her dress from her arms. Drawing the fabric over her head, he fanned her hair out on the pillow. She could tell the rumpled mess turned him on by the growing bulge in his slacks.

Before she could reach for him, he'd tugged his shirttails from his trousers and destroyed the garment himself. Hopefully it could be repaired. It had fit him perfectly, hugging his broad shoulders, which tapered to his trim waist in an inverted triangle of ridges and valleys that had her drooling.

Next he unbuckled his belt and yanked the leather from around his hips. He ditched it on the floor beside the bed, where he stood to shuck his pants before she could finish taking in the striking lines of his form. And when he paused, modeling his gray boxer briefs, she silently begged him to shove them off, revealing what looked to be some pretty impressive equipment.

"Ladies first." He caught her wide-eyed stare and grinned.

"You don't want the honors?" Linley decided to fight fire with fire. She fondled herself, first cupping her breasts in her hands, enhancing her cleavage by exaggerating the support of her bra. Then she rubbed down her abdomen to lay one hand over her pussy.

The mewl that burst from her throat surprised them both.

And pressed Chase into action.

He growled as he stalked nearer and divested her of the scrap of black lace protecting her mound before she could blink. Next he wedged his hand beneath her and flicked the clasp of her bra open faster than she could have done it herself. Clearly an expert, he peeled the lingerie from her shoulders. He lifted it from her chest as if it were the lid of a box housing an expensive present.

He scanned her naked body from her pink-painted

toenails to the waves at the end of her hair. Just when she thought he'd explode in a flurry of seductive motions, ramping their interlude up to the next level, he surprised her by backing off.

"Would you mind if I lit some of those candles?" The flick of his chin toward her mantle and the side tables helped her understand despite the fog in her brain.

"Of course not. Go ahead. There are matches in the dish beside the pillars."

Linley watched him stalk from cluster to cluster of the pretty votives, jars, and sticks. She adored candles of every variety.

Flame caught as soon as he touched the head to the striker. She could sympathize with the poor bit of tinder. He'd set her ablaze with as little effort. When he'd finished ringing them in the warm yellow glow of flickering light, he extinguished the overhead lamp and returned to their nest.

"Need some dim lighting to hide the imperfections?" The bit of disappointment winging through her didn't improve her mood. How could he have the ability to hurt her after just a few hours? Why did his opinion matter? She couldn't say, but it did.

Chase blinked at her. Then understanding dawned across his face with a grimace. "Are you kidding me, love?"

She reached for him but he'd already abandoned the bed, and her, once more.

"Does this look like I'm struggling to get in the game?" He shoved his thumbs beneath the waistband of his briefs then maneuvered the elastic over his bulging cock.

"Um." Something more coherent refused to come to mind. "Nope."

"Damn straight." His nostrils flared as he gave the long, thick erection a few strokes from root to tip. "More like I needed a time-out to collect myself. Pouncing on you and ravaging you like a Neanderthal isn't exactly my style. That's more Ryder's thing, if that's what you were hoping for."

"No, no. Sorry." She snorted when he rolled his eyes. "My mistake."

"I'm not opposed to convincing you of how much I like what I see." Lowering himself onto the bed again, he tucked himself into her open arms and descended until they were pressed together from head to toe—skin on skin.

Linley gasped.

He took the opportunity to kiss her, this time with more hunger than he'd allowed free rein before. The heavy shaft of his cock rested on her belly. If only he were inside her instead, she might be able to work off some of the pressure driving her mad.

"I think I need to teach you a lesson, love." He speared his fingers into her hair, fisting a handful of waves that he used to angle her head as he pleased. "About just how lovely I think you are."

"Does it involve you fucking me?" Her wistful tone had them sharing a laugh again. "I'm a quick learner if it does."

"Eventually." Chase delighted in her needy fidgeting beneath him. About the time she figured out how to position herself to rub against his corded thigh and grant herself a measure of release, he shifted. "No cheating. Bad girl."

Before she could object, he'd retreated. His hands spanned her waist as he flipped her over. Lying on her stomach, her face turned so that her cheek rested on the high-quality linens, she wriggled, knowing her ass was prominently displayed for him.

Still, she didn't expect the crack of his palm meeting her rounded flesh. The sound more than the corresponding sting made her flinch. And when the brief spark of pain fizzled into something warm and very pleasant, she sighed.

"You like that?" He had to be able to tell when she spread her legs for him, hoping to gain some relief for herself.

The rubbing of his finger over her slit from behind proved he hadn't missed the glistening arousal there. "Mmm."

"Say it." This time his directive didn't brook any argument.

Except that her overwhelming horniness made it hard to think. "What?"

"Tell me you know how gorgeous you are. That you can see how desperately I need you. That the slap of my palm on your ass makes you hotter than you could have imagined before tonight." Without pausing, he tortured her until she complied.

"Yes, yes, yes." She rocked her body back and forth as she uttered the word he teased from her. "Now, please, fuck me."

"Not sure you understand quite yet." Chase *tsked* at her. His grasp on her waist returned. But this time he didn't rotate her as she imagined he would. Instead he lifted, forcing her to bury her knees in the mattress to stay upright.

Again he treated her ass to several strong spanks that had to set his hand on fire as much as they did her ass. The shock of the answering desire that curled through her gut didn't lessen any. And neither did the sweet pleasure humming between her legs.

In fact, when he licked a path from her pussy damn near to her ass, she would have rocketed forward. Good thing his arm had banded around her waist to ensure she stayed immobile, directly in line with his talented tongue.

Linley dipped her head so that she could watch him from beneath her body. She spied him flip so that he reclined on his back with her pussy positioned over his open mouth.

"Come on, love." He guided her lower as he encouraged her. "Feed me the taste of you."

She squealed when her engorged tissue alighted on his mouth. Empowered, she drew on her experience as a leader in the business realm to inform her less-used inner vixen.

The power of his incredible finesse tempted her to shift until his attention maximized her pleasure. Before long, she rode his face with unabashed abandon.

His grunts and enthusiastic licking communicated his approval loud and clear.

So she gave him more of herself. Grinding onto his jaw, she felt the nudge of his nose on her clit along with the slide of his tongue across the folds of her pussy.

When he probed her opening, ringing the clenching portal with the tip of one long, thick finger, she rocked backward. The attempt to embed him failed when he withdrew temporarily.

Chase proved how generous he was being by permitting her the illusion of control. He lifted her several inches with a firm clasp on her hips.

"Tell me what you need." He nipped her thigh. She wondered how slick the skin there was given his recent foray. "I want to hear you beg, then scream as you come on my face."

She shivered in his hold.

He kept whispering naughty things to her, planting ideas in her lust-soaked mind. "And when you think you can't take any more, *that's* when I'll fuck you, love."

Then he dangled her just out of his reach. She squirmed, attempting to reconnect with the wet velvet heat of his mouth.

"Tell me." He shook her just enough to get her attention.

"Let me down. Please, I'd like more of your mouth on me." A flush burst over her chest, neck, and cheeks.

Chase's chuckle was strained with desire. "So polite, love. I'd like that too."

"Then quit teasing me, damn it. Lick me. Suck me. Bury your fingers inside me." Dirty talk burst from her with surprising ease when she was properly motivated.

"That's more like it." On a groan, he smothered himself with her passion.

Happy sighs floated from between her parted lips when they reconnected. Quickly, they morphed into needy moans.

Linley reached behind her, grabbing his hand, which splayed on her ass cheek. She squeezed, desperate to be filled in conjunction with the havoc his lips, tongue, and even teeth wreaked on her body.

Rapture built, tightening everything inside her until she feared she might fracture if he didn't relieve some of the mounting tension.

Chase didn't disappoint. At her nonverbal plea, he scooted his hand lower and began to seek out her moist center. When the tip of one finger sank inside an inch or two, she knew she wouldn't have long to enjoy the pleasure he imparted.

Soon she would implode.

"Please. Hurry, please." Linley dismissed the desperation in her entreaty. She didn't think her current vulnerability was a well-kept secret from either of them at this point.

His answering grunts as he invaded the tight sheath of her constrictive muscle gave her some reassurance she wasn't alone in the storm of passion whipping around them, tossing her body and emotions as if they were as insubstantial as a puff of cotton candy.

God knew this pleasure was sweet enough.

Chase suckled on her clit while another finger joined the first. This time he burrowed deeper, preparing her for the eventual invasion of his cock.

That thought alone instigated a clench. It rippled through her channel, hugging his embedded digits.

His hum of approval guaranteed he realized the impact of his manipulation.

Linley writhed, rubbing the aching peaks of her breasts

on the smooth, heated surface of the silk sheets below her. The potent mix of sounds, sensations, and the surreal victory of her escapade, had her drunk on the man between her thighs and what they'd managed to forge together.

Suddenly, the extent of her selfishness shamed her. The desire to impart even a fraction of that bliss in him spurred her to move. Or at least she attempted to dismount his busy mouth to return the favor.

The resounding smack he blessed her derrière with forced her closer instead of permitting her escape. Testing him, she squirmed again with the same result. Only his spank came harder this time.

Never could she have imagined the ecstasy the rougher-than-she-was-used-to contact could deliver. The impact of his strong palm infused her with additional heat that caused a meltdown in her core.

"Chase!" An attempt to warn him cut short when her entire being paused for several heartbeats as she hung suspended. And then she crashed. Or flew.

Linley lost track of her surroundings as she convulsed endlessly. Her fingers clenched in the sheets, rending the material for all she knew—or cared—at the moment.

The relief overpowered her until she collapsed bonelessly. Effortless laughter spilled from her lightened soul.

Chase wormed beside her so that their eyes were even. He gathered her to his chest and brushed stray locks from her face. "Well, that's a reaction I've never gotten before."

His adorable frown inspired her to pepper his face with kisses. When she covered his mouth and sampled their mingled flavor, she moaned.

Because, just like that, her libido shifted into overdrive like this had been a decadent pit stop. Unused for a while, parts of her begged for another go around on the Chase ride.

"Yeah?" He smiled as he toyed with her fingers.

"Again? So soon?"

"Uh huh." More explanation didn't seem necessary.

"Still feeling adventurous?" He grinned at her.

"Uh huh." They both laughed at her automatic reply. It was true.

"Good. Then I hope you don't mind this." Clearly he had the upper hand, not having his brain fogged by euphoria. The purpose of the lightning-fast move he made didn't register at first. Not until she realized she couldn't move her hands to pet his ripped chest and abdomen, which hovered in front of her face. By then he'd finished securing her wrists with the length of silk he'd worn around his neck not too long ago.

Linley had never been bound before, but the thrill of knowing she relied on him to guide their exchange had a trickle of arousal spilling down her thigh.

"You like that?" He smiled gently as he rubbed his thumb over her cheek.

"Uh huh." She winked.

"Brat." Chase reached over her once more to grab a condom from his pants. He tore the foil open carefully then rolled the thin latex over his hard-on in a flash. "We'll have to see what we can do about that. You seemed to like my hand on your ass. It's nice and pink. Begging for more."

He would know since he'd reset her on her knees, supporting her with an arm around her waist as he parked himself between her thighs. "I'm done waiting, Linley. I'm patient, but I'm not a saint. This is what you want too, yes?"

"Yes!" She shouted when he nudged her pussy with the tip of his cock.

And that was all the encouragement it took.

Chase penetrated her, gliding slowly and smoothly until he lodged within her. Then he worked his erection through her rings of muscle, tunneling a bit deeper with every pass. It seemed he'd grown since she'd spotted him last. The stretch of her pussy burned slightly. Only for a minute.

When he settled into his rhythm, she was sure it was her pace too. Never before had sex felt so perfect. In a matter of minutes, he had stoked her desire to inferno levels once more. She rested on her bound wrists, the tug of the tie only enhancing each of his lunges forward.

And when he smacked her ass in between two deep strokes within her, she knew she would come embarrassingly fast. Again.

"Don't wait on my account." He breathed hard between each word. "I'm with you, Linley. Any time. Every time, I hope."

The sweet promise…of *more*…collected all the glimmers of pleasure he gifted her with into one ball of bliss. Light touches on her shoulders and ass turned into something better when he dropped forward, blanketing her back as his pelvis slapped into her thighs. He reached around, one hand toying with her breasts while the other strummed her clit.

Unraveling in his arms, she was grateful for his embrace and the bindings holding her together through the monumental outpouring of their shared pleasure.

"Linley!" He grunted her name over and over as he emptied himself within her, each jerk of his hips timed to one of the answering wrings of her pussy around him. They came with wild abandon, similar to everything they'd done that night and hopefully would do many times more.

As the clenching of her pussy faded, she tried to dismiss the similar pump of another muscle, one much higher…in her chest.

To find out what happened next, turn to page 161, *Chase Epilogue.*

Linley Picked Ryder

To his credit, Ryder didn't gloat. The wide span of his smile made his slightly crooked front teeth visible. The imperfection endeared him to her. Whatever this man had achieved in his life, he'd blazed the path to success himself.

The part of her that had clawed its way to the top recognized its counterpart in him.

He draped his arm around her waist and tugged her against his side. Heat poured off his rock-solid torso, infusing her with warmth. Thank God the table prevented her from climbing into his lap right then and there.

That would have been embarrassing. Especially given the resigned shake of his head that Chase surrendered when he detected her instant capitulation to Ryder's allure.

"Sorry," she murmured. Neither of them deserved rejection. In five minutes they'd turned her on more than a year of pointless dates. "It wasn't any easy decision."

"Not a big surprise. Everyone loves to go wild their first time out of the gate." Chase smiled at her, sincere in his encouragement. "I don't blame you in the least. Don't be afraid. Ryder will take good care of you, even if he is an ass. And when you've got the initial rowdiness out of your system, you know where to find me."

"Don't hold your breath." Ryder chuckled. "It was good seeing you again."

"You too." Chase reached across the table to shake Ryder's outstretched hand. "We should grab a game again sometime soon."

"Definitely. Let me know when you're free and we'll see what we can do." The guys put her at ease with their sportsmanship. Underground clearly excelled at weeding would-be jackasses from their roster with extreme prejudice. "It was lovely to meet you." Chase leaned across the small table and dusted a kiss over her temple before slipping from the booth.

"Same goes." She smiled as he sauntered away. Before he'd even crossed to the wide doors on the other side of the space, a leggy blonde had approached and fawned at his side.

"No worries. That bastard will have plenty to distract him from his loss tonight." Ryder rolled his eyes, belying his tough-guy act. "The instant he sits at the piano in the library with a tumbler of the expensive whiskey he prefers, women fall all over him."

"Jealous?" She wondered.

"Hell no." He snorted. "I've got the sexiest lady here tonight. A new recruit at that. You know what they say… You never forget your first. It's considered a big honor to escort a newbie. So thank you."

Linley bit her lip. A little worried, she'd rather skip to the meat of the matter than dance around what she'd signed herself up for. If she waited too long, she might bail. "You're welcome. But would you mind if we don't chitchat too much before we get started?"

"Nothing to be nervous about, wildcat." Ryder turned her face toward him until she couldn't avoid his stare. "I've got you. I meant what I said before. I won't let you bite off too much. I may not be the smartest guy in the world, but I know this. If you're scared or not turned on, I'll pull us back to somewhere safer. Softer. Promise."

She nodded.

"But something tells me you're going to be pacing me, or maybe even keeping me on my toes. I'll be racing behind you once you really get started." He growled as if he could sense the fire lighting inside her.

The clash of their lips inspired her to take more. With Ryder, she didn't have to worry about propriety or being subtle. He granted her freedom from the restrictions of her daily life and all the bureaucratic bullshit she had to endure. No one had warned her about those trappings when she'd been in business school. Thank God or she might never have kept going.

Spearing her hands in his unruly hair, she dug deeper.

"That's right. You can get as dirty as you want with me." He nipped her bottom lip. "I'll only like it more."

Their tongues met and sparred. Champagne combined with something suspiciously like chocolate, making her moan at the taste. When they broke, she arched a brow at him. "You have a sweet tooth?"

"I'm here with you, aren't I?" He grinned when she slugged his shoulder. "But yes, if you must know, dark chocolate—preferably Belgian—is one of my many vices."

"Show me some others?" She nudged him toward the mouth of the booth.

"Of course." He scooped her from the bench seat and twirled her around enough to make her worried she flashed her black lace thong at some of the other guests, who smiled at the spectacle they made.

They marched down the hall, not pausing to investigate the inviting spaces of Underground. Linley did find herself distracted by the menagerie filling the black and white ballroom they skipped through, causing them to slow.

Her hand tugged on Ryder's where they were linked.

"Maybe after the edge is off, you'll dance with me?" He whirled her in circles and ground their pelvises together to the beat of The Wanted's "Glad You Came." He sambaed her in reverse through the crowd, displaying just a hint of his prowess on the floor.

Though she loved to dance, she didn't often get to indulge outside the privacy of her own master suite as she got dressed for the day ahead or unwound after the day behind. Sedate corporate gatherings didn't count.

"That sounds amazing." She couldn't help but notice the hardness he pressed against her belly. "Maybe while you're recovering."

"I like the way you think, Linley." Her name sounded dark and a little dirty when he said it like that. "Though it'll probably be just before dawn by the time I need more than a few minutes to get ready for another round with you." He leaned forward and bit her neck gently. "You do things to me."

"Good things, I hope." She laughed.

"Very." He pouted just a bit. "Can't you tell?"

"I assumed you're a rake with all the women you meet here." She dug her fingers into his pecs, loving the resistance of his toned muscles.

"True, true." His smile grew. "But usually I have a tiny bit more self-control. If it weren't against the rules, I'd probably already be fucking you right here on this floor."

"There are restrictions?" Suddenly she felt as if she were running full tilt in the dark. What did she know about where they were going or how to behave?

"Even paradise has rules, sadly." Ryder explained. "No sex in the main Underground. If being watched is your fantasy, that can be arranged easily. Right over there is the entrance to Downstairs. And if you make it through that decadent potluck without being distracted, there's plenty more to sample in the Basement."

Linley peeked over her shoulder. As much as she enjoyed being pressed to him on the dance floor, she knew there were far better places for them to be intimate. Besides, she wanted him naked so she could feel his skin against hers from head to toe.

"I don't want to wait anymore." A few steps later, he'd caught up to her, matching her determined strides.

"Been craving this for a while, huh?" He slung his arm around her shoulder and steadied her as they began to descend in unison.

"You have no idea." She sighed.

"You might be surprised," he murmured.

So unlike him, the tentative rebuttal had her pausing on the landing halfway down the grand staircase. "Seriously?"

"Yeah." He glanced away then back. "Sometimes circumstances in real life make it difficult to be who you really are inside. At least not without the fear of repercussions for you. Or your family."

The flex of his Adam's apple intrigued her almost as much as his cryptic comment. Secrets stayed private here, no matter how close she came to begging him for more details. After all, she knew the same was true for herself. If the media ever caught wind of this little foray into darkness, her image would be ruined and her company with it.

Scandal seemed to work for building the demand for celebrities. Not so much for CEOs.

"Hey." She laid her hand lightly on his broad shoulder. "I understand. I'm sorry you've had to put up with that crap."

His fingers blanketed hers and squeezed. When he spun around, his rogue's smirk had recovered. "So, what do you think of our lovely mural?"

It wasn't until he turned his palms upward that she took in the details of the warm colors swirling around them. Focused on the curtain at the bottom and the hints of flesh she glimpsed beyond, she'd missed the subject matter entirely.

"Wow." Her eyes bugged out a little as she monitored the saturnalia strewn about. "Some of these are pretty creative."

Ryder laughed again, the raucous sound playing with her insides, making them flip. She scanned the oil paintings of couples engaged in foreplay and sex of all flavors. The skill with which they'd been rendered ensured they were as gorgeous as they were raunchy.

The true art highlighted to her the fact that all the acts were natural. Fresh and honest expressions of one of life's greatest pleasures.

"Everything you see here is an option Downstairs." Ryder erased some of the space between them.

"Even that?" She pointed to a crowd of the pretty people gathered around a woman on her hands and knees. A man took her from behind. It might have been a trick of the light, but it appeared he really did take her behind.

Ryder choked on his sarcasm. "I'd be willing to sacrifice for you, wildcat. Sure."

Her eyes went wide. Embarrassed to admit she'd considered the possibility, she blushed because the thought didn't completely repulse her. "Does it feel good?"

"If I do it right." His shoulders broadened as his chest puffed up. "I've been told I'm not a slouch at pleasing my women. I can be smooth when it's called for."

A woman passing by stumbled then turned toward them. "Honey, you have no idea how good you've got it tonight. He's being ridiculously modest."

"Don't rat me out, Eva." Ryder cleared his throat.

"Trust me." The woman pointed at Linley's guy for the evening. "He's never lonely around here. Enough said. Enjoy."

"I will." Linley nodded at the retreating guest.

He whistled innocently, as if he hadn't overheard the entire exchange.

"Quite a reputation, sir." She pinched his arm to get his attention.

"Careful, wildcat." He growled against her neck from where he'd swallowed her in his embrace. "Power exchanges with a little sensual pain tossed in are one of my favorite ways to play."

The solid erection he sported proved his promise. Steely and thick, he made her long to cut to the chase. "Show me the rest."

"Greedy." He stole another drugging kiss before smiling against her lips. "I approve."

"Thanks," she muttered.

"But you're not quite ready—"

"I am!" The assertion escaped before she could stop it.

"I'll keep that in mind." His voice turned gravelly. "I was referring to your clothes, though. Once we pass the curtain, there's a dress code. Or maybe an *undress* code is a better term."

"Oh." Again she'd flashed her naiveté.

"I get the sense you didn't head out with this in mind. So you have some options. You can leave your dress and shoes at the coat check if you like your underwear well enough. Or you can strut around naked, which I highly recommend." The selfish smirk reemerged. "If neither of those options appeal, there are some branded items you can take from the lockers in the corner over there. You would make a hell of an advertisement for anything sexy, this place especially."

"I'll stick with my own lingerie, thanks." She refused to think about it as parading around in her underwear. Thank God she'd worn something hot. Just in case…

They continued until they were beside the storage area. An attendant nodded to Ryder, who didn't hesitate to strip his fitted black T-shirt over his head. She was almost too entranced by the landscape of his pecs and defined abs to notice when he shucked his shoes and socks.

Leather whipped through the loops on his jeans when he removed his belt. With it curled over his knuckles, he made her knees weak. But it was when he unzipped the denim and revealed his bare hard-on that she nearly had a heart attack.

"Close your mouth or I'll give you something to suck on." His smile softened the command, though part of her imagined he wasn't entirely joking.

"You're…" She licked her lips. "Whoa."

There went that laugh again. Rich and boisterous. It ensnared her heart a bit more every time she brought it out of him.

"Thanks." He brushed the pad of his thumb across her dampened mouth. "Your turn."

Linley's fingers fumbled at her hem. Could she do this? No one else seemed particularly disturbed by the gorgeous, very naked man in their ranks. What would it matter if there was an almost-nude woman joining him?

Other than the fact that she'd never been so bold.

Sure, she'd had lovers. Not many, and none she'd stripped for outside the dim light of their bedroom. Plus, that had been years ago. In her college days. Before she'd gotten rusty and the stakes had climbed so high.

She needed to find that old sense of adventure and have some fun.

"Do I need to help you?" He clasped the edge of her dress in his strong hands and walked it up her thighs. He hummed when the tiny triangle of lace covering her waxed mound came into view. "Very pretty, Linley. I can see your wetness decorating them from here."

She whipped her gaze to the attendant, who feigned disinterest as he stared across the lobby.

"Show me your tits." Ryder took her hand in his and lifted it to where he'd gotten her started. The stroke of his fingers over his erect shaft emboldened her. He certainly liked what he saw so far. There was no lying about that.

Like ripping off a hangnail, she opted for quick. No way to take it back when she whipped her dress over her head and thrust it at the suddenly ready attendant. Bored her ass.

"Damn, you're gorgeous." The scorching laser of Ryder's gaze swept her from head to toe then made a return journey.

"No, I'm horny." She practically panted. "Don't make me wait much longer. Please."

She might have imagined the attendant's muttered, "Jesus." She didn't think so, though.

"Come." Ryder snagged her hand and led her toward the curtain. "You're killing me."

"Me?" She concentrated on evening her respiration. "You're the one strutting around like a sex god."

The smile that spread slowly across his face rewarded her plenty for her honesty.

"Thank you, Linley. Let's make this tour fast so you can pick your pleasure."

"I'm fairly sure that as long as I'm with you, tonight is going to be unforgettable." She lifted their joined hands and kissed his knuckles.

"Ditto, wildcat." They burst through the curtain to Downstairs perfectly in synch.

All around them, sensuality abounded. Couples clung on furniture of all varieties. They clustered around pairs actively engaged in intercourse of all shapes and sizes. Plenty of men or women treated their counterparts to oral pleasure as they observed others or were the focus of attention.

Ryder didn't hesitate. He led her toward the back of the room, past a row of doorways. They were marked with various fantasies. The Toy Chest. Peeping Toms, Vanilla, The Grotto, Costumes 'R Us, and Ties That Bind

Each had a vacant or occupied light illuminated on the front. They went on for as far as she could see until the portals turned a corner. She didn't doubt as many or more lurked around the bend.

Naked waitresses and equally buff waiters served the clientele when they needed refreshments. All around her the sounds of sex reverberated.

Imagining herself in place of the woman draped over a sofa while her partner devoured her caused her to stumble. Ryder had her wrapped in his arms in no time. Instead of letting her go, he lifted her and carried her effortlessly across the room.

A dark spiral staircase made of something that looked like ebony caught her eye...and her imagination.

"You've gotten a glimpse at what you can expect Downstairs." Ryder cupped her sex as he spoke, distracting her with the promise of what he'd show her next. "But the Basement is a whole new level of fun."

More than this?

She craved knowing what that might be like but couldn't imagine something better.

"You can have multiple partners. I have friends. I'd give you that." He whispered to her between nibbles on her ears and neck. "Or bondage. Have you ever wanted to be tied up, Linley?"

Her knees wobbled but he steadied her, impaling her on several of his fingers at once. "Maybe. But... Didn't we pass a room for that here?"

"Yes. Ties That Bind is a lighter version of the cuffs, shackles, spreader bars, and bondage equipment you'll find in the Basement." Ryder smiled. "I like it all. If you want to test-drive the place first, I'm fine with that. I know you'll be back for more."

"Like what?" Linley could hardly breathe past the anticipation strangling her.

"There are rooms for all sorts of fetishes." He promised her the world and everything below it. "I'll take you wherever you'd like to go. What's between us won't change. This heat. Damn it, I like you Linley. Tell me what will make you happy."

She blinked back unexpected tears at his generosity and his ferocity. The same washed over her. Intending to please him in return, she considered.

"Pick quickly. I can't wait much longer." He growled. "Do you want me to play with you here? Or should I take you to the Basement?"

If Linley picked *Play Downstairs,* turn to page 17, *Play Downstairs.*

If Linley picked *The Basement* turn to page 38, *Take Me To The Basement.*

Toy Chest With Chase

"The Toy Chest is open," Linley whispered. A shiver ran through her.

"Hell, yes." The pressure of his fingers on her cheek tipped her face toward him. Chase stole a deep kiss. He ended the sweet yet dirty meeting of their mouths prematurely. "Come on, before someone beats us to it."

They practically hurdled the couch in their haste to abscond to the fantasy chamber. When they drew up short in front of the elaborately carved hardwood, Chase paused with his hand on the knob.

"No second guessing here." She answered before he could ask. "Let's do this. Show me what's behind that door."

"You got it." He laughed at her eagerness. Not in a mean way, but with an indulgent partner-in-crime sort of flavor.

They held hands as he pushed the panel open and drew her inside, closing them in darkness together. When he slid the dimmer up gradually, she gasped.

The room was the stuff of erotic daydreams. Burnished silver accents offset the deep purple of the walls. A gorgeous oval mirror reflected her stunned expression and Chase's undivided focus on her reaction.

He smiled as she discovered the nuances of the chamber.

Armoires and dressers lined each available space on the perimeter other than an extra-wide armchair. A low, tufted bench stretched across the foot of an enormous four-poster bed, complete with a draped, silk canopy.

Silver and purple sheets were perfectly made and a whole host of pillows called to her, inviting her to crash into their fluffiness. Naked. With this amazing, sexy, sophisticated guy who seemed to be as enthralled by her as

91

she was with him.

What more could she want?

Oh, right. Toys.

An enormous smile spread across her face.

"I love that look. Angelic and devilish all at once."
Chase bent to kiss her grin. He started off slow and gentle,
but before she knew it, he had her balanced in his arms. Her
legs were wrapped around his waist, allowing her to feel
every inch of him against her mound and belly. The habitual
sway of her torso rubbed her breasts on his chest.

Just when she might have said the hell with it all and
begged him to make love to her—the plain vanilla variety—
he set her on the cool polished surface of one of the armoires.
She yelped then squirmed. He ensured she didn't tumble off
with a sure grip on her waist.

"Stop distracting me, love." He brushed his thumb over
her swollen mouth. "Let me show you the possibilities before
you dissolve my concentration."

"I wasn't complaining," she reminded him.

"True. But when you leave here tonight, I want you to
have everything you came for." His eyes went soft, and she
wished she could hug him.

"I've already found more than I expected," she
promised.

"But what about all you wished?" He refused to fall
short. "*That's* the least I'll permit."

Linley ducked her head, using the cascade of her hair to
camouflage the mist that caused a sheen over her eyes. How
could she have gotten so lucky?

If Chase wasn't fooled, he remained a gentleman, giving
her time to recover by angling away and busying himself
with intricate latches on the set of dressers beside her. He
flipped up lids, opened cabinets, and drew out drawers to
reveal their contents.

To call the collection in the Toy Chest extensive

wouldn't have done it justice. Some of the items were complete mysteries to her. She blinked. Several times. "What're you thinking, love?" He prodded gently. "I guess I'm a lot more naive than I thought." A blush stole over her cheeks. "I was imagining vibrators and maybe some handcuffs."

"There are plenty of those in here." He crossed to the largest of all the storage units and parted the doors on the front. Row after row of naughty paraphernalia in sealed, original packaging had her shifting on her fancy perch.

Vibrators, dildos, remote controlled clitoral stimulators—all the basics in every permutation were available for trial.

"The best part of this room is that is comes with souvenirs. You can pick three things. Anything we use is yours to keep, of course." Chase wiggled his eyebrows as he selected an enormous dildo in sparkly blue gel. The monster had more in common with his forearm than the generous yet realistic proportions of his natural equipment.

A laugh tumbled from Linley. She adored his ability to erase her awkwardness and trepidation. "Something tells me that's not on the recommended agenda for beginners like me."

"Love, I'm not sure a hundred years of practice could work you up to that thing." He tossed it back into place.

"Would you mind if we stuck to the stuff in the middle there?" She prayed he wouldn't be disappointed when she pointed to the tamer toys.

"What's that sour face for?" He crossed to her, standing between her legs while he surveyed the concern in her eyes.

"Am I boring to a guy like you?" She canted her head. "How can tonight be as exciting for you as it is for me when I'm hardly out of training wheels when it comes to sex?"

"Linley, corrupting you might be the most fun I've had in my entire life." His wicked grin reappeared. "Stop worrying. Don't think. Rely on your gut. Pick three items from that chest, right now."

"What will you do then?" She nibbled her cheek as she tested her ability to rile him. Surprisingly, it seemed to be true. She could affect him.

Chase dropped his head back. A groan burst from his throat.

"I'm going to demonstrate their effective use on your hot little body. Don't expect me to go easy on you since you're teasing me like a pro. You can ask me any questions you have, love." He surrounded her with his arms, drawing her to his chest and kissing her shoulder lightly beside the strap of her expensive French bra. "I want you to make an informed decision."

Linley shivered. Chase eased her from the armoire and set her on the floor near the beginner chest she'd indicated. She ran her fingers over several packages. Her first choice was a no-brainer. She'd always wanted to try this. After all, she'd heard women rave about using them on TV and in movies for years.

"These seem interesting. Which one do you recommend?" She appraised the selection of rabbit vibrators.

Chase hummed. "Very good taste. I mean you did pick me so we already knew that, but you're confirming my suspicions."

She elbowed him lightly in the ribs.

"Okay." He laughed. "Sorry. So when it comes to rabbits, there are a few standard features. Mostly they're your run-of-the-mill vibrator with some serious upgrades integrated into the design."

Linley leaned in for a closer view as he pointed to one in particular.

The pink shaft had a translucent section. A bulge in the shaft was filled with tiny marbles.

"When you turn it on, that part rotates. It'll tease you

inside with the shifting motion of the plastic pearls, right on your G-Spot. Plus, the swirling shaft will simulate intercourse since you'll probably trap it deep within you to maximize the contact of the actual rabbit with your clit." He pointed to a protrusion from the base of the tool.

She hadn't realized the silly character actually served a purpose. Well, that made a lot more sense and relieved her guilt over getting nasty with something so cute.

"I hear the magic is all in the ears. They're light and fluttery enough to feel like a tongue when they get slick," Chase murmured in her ear.

"All right. Yes. That." She could hardly catch her breath.

"Unless I'm stealing some of your fun."

Another blush heated her cheeks. This had to be a record for a single evening.

"Watching you unravel will be plenty reward. Plus, I'm man enough to admit you can take a hell of a lot more in one night than I can give you. Unless I start popping some recreational Viagra." He didn't have to elaborate for her to be sure cheating wasn't his style.

"If you're sure…" She glanced at him over her shoulder, meeting his smoldering stare.

"Love, does it seem like I disapprove?" He pressed his pelvis tighter to her lower back. Mistaking his excitement would have been impossible.

"You've been so kind to me tonight." She couldn't wait to kiss him again. "You pick one, please?"

"I'm a nice guy, but who could turn down an offer like that?" He looked like a kid in a candy shop. It didn't take more than a few seconds before he plucked a thin device from the chest.

It wasn't longer than her thumb and probably just about as thick. Stacked beads decreased in dimension along its length.

Linley tried to disguise her disappointment. After the

rabbit, this toy would be insubstantial. It didn't seem to move or anything either, though it had a U-shaped hook at one end that looked like it would prevent it from slipping completely inside her.

"It's not what you think, love." Chase laughed softly. So much for her poker face. He saw right through it—through her anxiety to her anticipation. "It's for your ass. Has anyone ever played with it?"

"Oh." She blinked. "No."

"We'll fix that then. You'll come so hard around me with this inside you. Just wait. So, what's your last pick for tonight?"

She considered chickening out. What was the point of that after she'd come so far?

"These." She slipped a finger beneath the silver chain connecting two metallic clothespins. At least that's what they resembled to her. "They *are* what I think, right?"

He chuckled. "Yes, love."

His tone had her confused when he plucked then from her and returned them to their place.

"You don't—"

He silenced her with a finger over her lips. "Nothing to do with me. Those are too harsh for you to start with."

Relief swamped her when he nominated a similar toy, both because he had her best interests at heart and because his triumphant smile proclaimed exactly how delighted he was with her selections.

"Your nipples will thank me," he promised. With that prophecy, he scooped her and their accoutrements into his arms before dashing to the bed. Despite his haste, he lowered her gently to the plush surface, then climbed on beside her, toying with the edge of her underwear. "Are you tired of these yet?"

"Amen."

Chase pounced on her with the reflexes of a hungry

predator. He whisked the lace from her lower body without any assistance from her. Her bra followed close behind.

Then he rocked back and knelt, sitting on his haunches while he observed her as if committing every curve of her body to long-term memory.

"You're even more lovely than I imagined." As if he didn't quite believe she was really there, he trailed a finger over her arm, then her collarbone, then her breast.

He plumped her nipples between his thumbs and forefingers until each turned a bold raspberry hue and grew tight.

The zings he sent to her pussy were like live wires making her dance beneath his intense caresses. The instant reaction of her body to his direction made her feel like an impish marionette. Glad to follow his lead, she reclined, granting him full access to do as he pleased.

Her eyelids must have drifted closed because she didn't see the lightweight nipple clamps in his hands.

But she felt their pleasant pressure when he applied them to the hard tips he'd created with his skillful handling. The cool metal enhanced the bulk of the nubs clasped in their adjustable hold.

"How do you feel?" Chase toyed with the shiny chain draped between her breasts, across the bottom of her rib cage.

A moan supplied all the answer he needed.

"They're not numb, right?" He instructed her on the use of the clamps. "For now we only want them snug, no tingles... Well, maybe just a few of the pleasurable kind."

"Check." She'd been reduced to one word sentences.

"Good girl." He sank over her, capturing her mouth in a fierce kiss that belied his gentle tutelage. The slab of his chest mashed the clamps enough to make her aware of them all over again. For a long time they were content to play, relishing the taste of each other. Licks, nips and moans were exchanged along with roaming caresses.

All too soon, Linley grew restless.

Chase noticed her escalating moans. "You're ready to try something else?"

"More." She craved additional sensation. Something to appease the demands of her body.

"No problem." He pressed a final kiss to her lips then meandered down her torso, testing the fit and impact of her unconventional jewelry. Approving, he continued.

When his face was level with her pussy, he grabbed the vibrator near her hip. He shredded the packaging and freed the poor critter who'd been trapped inside.

The bed dipped as Chase departed the cozy nest. She whimpered and reached for him before thinking better of the display of weakness.

"Coming right back, love." He rummaged in a drawer marked *Supplies*. "I need a few essentials. Like condoms. And lube."

"Are you nuts?" The question popped out. "I'm wet enough to drown that poor bunny."

He laughed. "The lubrication was for your ass, love. Trust me. You don't want to attempt that dry. Especially not your first time. Let's make it good so you want to do it again and again.

The man had a point. She shivered as he returned to her side.

"So tense." He petted her belly.

"Don't tell me to relax when you're about to put something up there." She grimaced, half-worried and half-excited.

He laughed the bright sound she was coming to adore. "It really does help the process along. But this is a beginner device. It's not going to be a big production. I promise."

Oddly, she trusted him one-hundred percent.

"That's better," he cooed. "This should help some too." Before she could raise her head to spy on his intent, the squishy, blunt tip of the vibrator pressed on her pussy's entrance. A moderate buzz followed a moment later. "Oh!" The immediate responsive clench of her entire body didn't seem to further his agenda. But after a minute, she sank into the experience. Her body sighed and accepted the toy's shaft, which he fed her inch by inch.

"There you go." He massaged her thighs and belly as he introduced the full length.

Moans slipped from her lips until the juncture of the vibrator and the clit stimulator nestled into place.

Then she shouted.

Her pussy hugged the intrusion as the external spurring served its purpose.

"Doing great, love." Chase grounded her through each exponential upgrade in rapture. "Now, let's see about my selection, shall we?"

"Ugh." Anything more substantial wouldn't coalesce in her mind.

Chase dropped soft kisses on her stomach, distracting her as he ripped open the anal toy and coated it with slick gel.

No amount of gentling would do the trick when he made first contact between the cool substance and the blaze of her skin.

She squealed.

He murmured reassurance. When she released her pent-up breath, he guided the toy into her the barest bit, as if waiting for her to object.

Who would refuse such delicious torture?

Chase plied her physical form with expert care and her primal emotions with his quiet command. The modest bulges of his toy slid into her ass, forcing it to alternately spread then relax. Foreign, the sensation was pleasantly arousing.

She shivered, embarrassed by how ridiculously easy it was for him to poise her on the verge of surrender.

"Oh, none of that." He refused to grant her quarter.

"Show me how much you like the way I play with you."

When he put it like that, it seemed a shame not to comply with his wishes. Especially when he winked at her before flicking the base of the vibrator.

"Chase!" She screamed when he triggered the internal gyration of the device. Her rhythmic motions rocked the clamps at her breast, pressed her onto the toy in her ass, and allowed the rabbit's ears to tap her clit.

He conducted the trio of rapture like a sexual maestro.

Linley exploded. She reached for him, thrilled to have his hand grounding her while she came apart.

"I've got you," he promised her over and over as she unraveled. All the while, she stared into his gorgeous blue eyes, and he returned the gaze.

"No." She shook her head when he smiled gently and kissed her with aching tenderness. "Don't slow down."

"Rest a minute, love." He swiped a damp strand from her lightly perspiring forehead. "We have all night."

She didn't care to waste an instant of their time together. "No."

Chase kissed the tip of her nose. "You're sure you're ready for me after that?"

"Now, please," she begged.

"Who am I to deny a lady?" He beamed as he reached between her legs and eased the vibrator from its den.

She hadn't even noticed him flick it off.

Before she could miss the pressure filling her, he was replacing it with something better.

Bigger. Wider. Longer. Hotter.

And when he fused them completely, it felt as though he'd introduced her to more than playing with toys or a libertine club.

Chase showed her just how good sex could be with the right person. She spread her legs, welcoming him deeper within her on every pass.

"Linley," he grunted her name.

She understood and hugged him to her as he finally took for himself, giving her so much satisfaction in return.

His chest triggered sparks in her breasts when he bumped the clamps, and his cock stroked the plug through the thin tissue separating him from the anal beads.

"Come with me?" she whispered her request.

Clenching his teeth, he nodded.

Linley gasped as his lips crashed onto hers and his hips fucked faster. She couldn't say who came first, but suddenly they both had lost control and shuddered in counterpoint to each other.

When she swore she'd die from the ecstasy bombarding her, it lessened and resolved into sweet, warm relief.

To find out what happened next, turn to page 161, *Chase Epilogue*.

Happiest At Home

Linley wrung her hands as she glanced between Chase and the velvet curtain separating her from the official Downstairs.

"If you have to think that hard, that's answer enough." Chase smiled warmly, letting her off the hook. "There's always next time."

She swallowed and nodded, thankful for his graceful perceptiveness.

"It's true what you said," she explained. "I didn't come here because I wanted to go crazy tonight. It's more that my life makes casual encounters impossible outside a place like this. There are always...expectations. Now that I've met you, I'd rather continue our night somewhere quiet. Comfortable. Private."

"Believe me. I completely understand that desire." He squeezed her shoulder then swept his palm along her arm until he entwined their fingers. "I'm sort of glad to have you to myself without a million distractions. I don't date much. Not in the traditional sense. It would be a treat to hang out on your couch and watch a movie or talk over a cup of coffee."

"That does sound nice." Her heart melted a bit when he broke their stare to kiss her knuckles.

"Do you mind if I drive us?" He tugged her up the stairs, and she was all too happy to follow. His trim hips and tight butt—packaged in stylish trousers—drew her attention.

"Linley?" He tried not to grin when he caught her spying on his assets.

"Hmm?" She did her best imitation of innocence.

"I was wondering if you'd ride with me. It's getting late, and I'd rather travel together." The caress of his thumb over her wrist didn't help her concentration.

She almost objected. She could look out for herself, and her car was her baby. Abandoning it in the concrete bowels of Underground didn't appeal. A few minutes alone to sort out her thoughts might not hurt either. Then she realized showing off would reveal an awful lot about her she'd rather not discuss. In fact… "Crap!"

Where are we going to have this little rendezvous? Certainly not at her main house. The enormous glass windows of the mansion overlooking the valley that rambled down to the ocean wouldn't do. No, she'd take him to her cottage on the outskirts of the city. Her thinking place.

"Don't worry." He misunderstood. "Underground will deliver your car to your house later. It's a common service they provide."

"Makes sense." She cleared her throat. "I'd like to come back sometime. They've thought of everything. But I'm the kind of person who'd enjoy the experience more with someone I trust."

"I hope you'll put me in that category eventually. I'm not opposed to earning the honor." He clasped her hand tighter.

"Sorry. That sounded rude." Linley couldn't believe how accommodating Chase had been. And she returned the favor with unintentional backhanded remarks.

"No. It came off as pragmatic." He escorted her through the ballroom then along the hall toward the garage. "I like that about you. You're careful and smart. Sure of yourself because you think things through."

"I have to tell you, it's pretty attractive when you read my mind." She snuggled up to his chest when they approached the booth and a young, stylish man jogged out toward the sea of cars after nodding at Chase. The attendant obviously recognized him. Just how much of a pillar was he at Underground? And what did it say that he was willing to leave for her? With her. "I'm not sure I've ever met someone else who gets me like you do."

"Maybe that's because we're a lot alike. Here... You're chilly." He buffed her arms before separating them just enough to shrug off his jacket and wrap it around her. She hugged the fine fabric to her, more to surround herself with the heat and scent of the man she couldn't believe she'd only met an hour ago. He seemed so *familiar*.

Even if she'd run a fever of one hundred and five, she wouldn't have stopped him from bundling her in his arms. He leaned his cheek on the crown of her head and breathed deep.

Linley settled against him. The thickness of his erection prodded the small of her back.

She hadn't realized she'd gasped until he apologized. "Underground usually has that effect on me. I guess I've been conditioned. And tonight, adding you to the mix... There's no hope of hiding that."

"I don't mind. I like knowing where I stand with you." Understatement of the century. Actually, she had to refrain from rubbing against him like a cat on the edge of a doorframe.

"Good. Because I'm fairly certain it's going to be a regular occurrence when we're together." He kissed her cheek. "*If* you'll let me see you again after tonight."

"Why wouldn't I?" Their lips brushed when she turned to look at him from the corner of her eye.

"Because—" He hesitated.

"What?" She rotated in his arms so she could cup his smooth cheek.

When he closed his eyes for a moment then reopened them, the somber look in them disappeared. "I guess I was afraid you had come here tonight looking for a one-time fling."

"I might have." She didn't intend to lie to him. It wasn't

her style. "But that was before I knew this was an option."
Even with the extreme heel of her shoe, she had to reach
up to nudge him lower so that they could nibble on each
other again. She might have been content to stay there
forever, but the headlights of an approaching vehicle shined
directly on them, blinding her. Or was that a reflection of the
electricity sparking between them?

"Hold that thought." He nuzzled their noses then led her
to the passenger side of the charcoal gray Mercedes Benz
E550 sedan that idled at the curb. Understated elegance. Just
like the man himself.

Somewhere along the way, she'd become a car snob. She
freely admitted it. The lucrative nature of her business had
allowed her to develop an appreciation for superior
machines. A man's ride told a lot about him. This one would
do nicely.

Linley slid into the comfortable leather seat and allowed
Chase to shut the door for her before reaching for her seat
belt. She ran her hand over the quality stitching and the well-
designed curve of the dash.

"You approve?" His half smile kicked up as he ducked
into the cabin and joined her.

"I do." She nodded. "I have to warn you, though. I'm
one of the world's worst passengers. Backseat driving is a
bad habit of mine."

"I'm sensing a theme here." He glanced at her before
putting the car in gear and smoothly ascending the winding
ramp. They emerged into the night. Stars shone, even in the
heart of the city. Out on the fringes of civilization, the
twinkles would be brilliant. She couldn't wait to share the
view with Chase. "So let me ask you this… If you like the
driver's seat so much, why are you letting me take charge?"

"Maybe I'm tired of navigating. Especially alone." She
scrubbed her hands over her face, careful to avoid streaking
the makeup she rarely wore so heavily.

"Fair enough." Chase reached across the cabin to rest his palm on her thigh. Not in a grope-o-rama way, but in a show of support. "Except I actually do need you to tell me where to go right now."

They laughed together, the sound filling the sedate interior.

"Head out to the highway then take Route 9 North. My place is kind of far. I hope you don't mind." She bit her cheek as penance for the half-truth.

"Not a problem. It only means I get to spend more time with you." Chase shot her a look filled with desire.

Fanning her face, she couldn't believe how warm the evening air felt. Or probably that had something to do with her flush, courtesy of the man beside her. She was dying to ask him things she knew were forbidden, questions she couldn't give a reciprocal answer to without impacting their night. So she kept her mouth closed and admired his skill in handling the vehicle instead.

Shoulders relaxed, his gaze flicked from the mirrors to the road. He maneuvered around slower vehicles without hogging the passing lane. Thank God. She couldn't stand left-lane pirates that parked themselves in the fast track at one mile *under* the speed limit no matter how many other vehicles approached.

That would have been a deal breaker.

"So, how am I doing?" The grin he shot her before concentrating on the road again proved they still rode the same wavelength.

"Not bad." A giggle escaped her when she covered his hand. "And you have a big gearshift."

"You haven't seen anything yet." The corner of his mouth curled up, creating a slight dimple. "Although, the real version isn't quite so shiny."

Chrome peeked between his tan fingers. The idea of him with a silver-plated cock had her laughing some more.

"I should hope not. I prefer men to robots." Linley shook her head when he choked. "Let me guess, that's another specialty of Underground."

"Well, actually." He glanced at her. "Yeah. There are fuck machines in the Basement."

It did something to her insides to hear him curse so naturally. A reminder that he might not always be as gentle as the treatment he'd given her so far. She shivered—part anticipation, part wariness. "Thanks, but no thanks. I want a flesh and blood man. Not that I indulge in those very often either. Suddenly, I have a pretty big craving though."

"Does that mean you still plan to take tonight beyond that coffee you promised me?" The inquiry didn't feel like pressure. More like curiosity.

"I think so." She nibbled her bottom lip and shifted in her seat. "It's been a really long time for me. Can we see where this goes and how it feels?"

"Absolutely." His shoulders relaxed. "I already know it'll be great. Nothing to worry about there. Forget a long time. I've *never* had this kind of chemistry with a woman before. You fit me, Linley."

"Well we don't know that yet, do we?" A blush stole across her cheeks after rushing up her chest and neck.

"I'll prove it to you later." The intensity of his promise distracted her enough to almost miss their exit.

"Shoot. It's this one. Sorry." She instinctively checked over her shoulder as he glided through several lanes, onto the ramp. Quick reflexes, awareness of his surroundings, and familiarity with the limits of his vehicle ensured he delivered them safely. His unshakeable calm put her at ease.

The chaos of her life would overwhelm a lot of people. Chase would be able to handle it. She didn't doubt that for a second. Should she tell him a little bit about her? She'd never had a one-night stand before and didn't intend to start at this point in her life. What if she fell into bed, into lust, and into something like infatuation with a man who wouldn't be interested in her once she revealed her identity?

"Left or right at the light?" He broke her from her internal debate.

"Right, thanks."

"You know, you could share what's on your mind." Without taking his eyes from the road, he played it cool.

"I'd rather not ruin the moment. Tonight is for fun, right?" She slipped her cell phone from a pocket sewn discreetly in her dress.

"It can be for whatever you like, Linley." He peeked at the screen she tapped. "What do you have there?"

"My phone. It's how we're going to get through the gate. Around this corner there's a tall hedge. Slow down and turn in by the stone pillar." Extending her wrist as they neared, she allowed the gadget to align with the sensor's range.

"Wow. Are you really Batgirl?" He wiggled his brows. "I always had a thing for superwomen."

"Hardly." A laugh burst from her, though his assessment probably hit nearer the mark than he could know. "I do have a thing for toys, though."

"I wish you'd confessed that before we left the stashes at Underground behind." Chase sighed. "We're definitely going to have to take another trip there someday."

The wrought iron parted, admitting them to the property. Although the simple structure utilized clean lines and a quaint charm she'd adored on first sight, the appointments were still high quality. Henry had personally attended to the security, which meant it outshone the needs of an average woman's home. Hopefully it didn't look too suspicious.

Chase parked on the cobblestone near the garage. When she would have joined him in the driveway, he wrapped his fingers around her wrist. "Stay there. I'll come get you."

Chivalry could feel oppressive, but not when he doled it out.

He assessed her through the windshield as he rounded the hood then reached in to hand her out of the car. "I like that look."

"I'm glad since you're easy on my eyes." She accepted his quick kiss before allowing him to walk her up the stone and turf pathway to the front door.

"I know the feeling, love."

A rustle came from the wildflower bed beside them. Before she could catch a glimpse of the trespasser, Chase had her tucked behind him. Feet spread shoulder width apart, knees slightly bent, he faced the offender. As a living barrier between her and whatever lurked in the bushes, he impressed her with both his protective instincts and his lightning grace.

If she were ever in trouble, she wouldn't mind having him by her side. In this case, she laughed then rubbed the tension from his impressive shoulders. "Calm down. It's only Mr. Hoppers. That's his favorite spot. The lawn guy tells me he's ruining the landscape. I don't mind though. He's pretty adorable."

"A rabbit? I think I can handle one of those." He glanced over his shoulder at her. "You don't have any guard dogs inside, do you?"

"Nah." A horrible pet parent, she didn't mention her two kitties safely ensconced in the hilltop home where she spent most of her non-work hours. The burn of omissions started to steal some of her joy. Is this what she really wanted? A night she could never repeat?

"Just teasing, Linley. I actually really like animals." He took her hand and started them up the two rock-hewn stairs to her porch. "I work late a lot, so I've limited myself to an aquarium for now, though."

"Really? Fresh or saltwater?" She paused with her hand at the pinpad on her doorframe.

"Actually I have one of each. I like the live plants and other fun stuff—like shrimp and snails—in my freshwater tank, but the colors of the fish and corals in my saltwater tank are incredible." The pause that followed made her wonder if he censored himself too.

Linley tried to hide her frown by concentrating on the lock mechanism. "They are very beautiful. There's a giant setup in the lobby of…my…office building. I swear I see something different each time I pass by."

"They're relaxing, too." He stroked his fingers through her hair as if to diffuse her mounting tension through manual intervention.

To give her privacy to type in her security code, Chase turned toward her more fully. His position allowed her to discreetly place her thumb on the fingerprint reader, which had the door swinging open. She looked at him with a smile designed to invite him across her threshold.

The impact of his attention hit her full force.

"Chase…"

"Don't whisper to me in that sexy tone if you're still hoping we can hold off long enough for you to brew that drink you wanted to share." He cleared his throat and backed her through the doorway and against the wall inside it. "I'm not used to waiting for what I want."

"Me either." She gulped as he trailed fingers across the bare skin at the top of her chest, parallel to the neckline of her dress.

"And this…?" The chain of kisses he laid down her neck nearly had her forgetting what he asked. "Is this what you had in mind?"

"Yes." She squeaked when he kicked the door closed, locked it, then scooped her into his arms.

"No reason we can't both have our wish then. Which way to your bedroom?" The growled question came in sections between languid kisses he dropped on her lips. Draped against his chest, she swore she could hear his heart pounding. Or perhaps that was her own.

Unable to pause long enough to inform him of the direction, she caressed his cheek, testing the faint scratch of his five-o'clock shadow. Then she drew herself up and reclaimed his lips.

He groaned as his tongue slipped out to tease the seam of her smile. Allowing him entrance, she parted her lips and was rewarded by the gentle probing of his wet, silky skin on hers. Totally engrossed in the gentle nips and licks, she didn't realize he'd ferreted out her sleeping space until he lowered her to the plush duvet.

Chase swiped his jacket from beneath her, folding it over the arm of a wingback chair in the corner. He slid her shoes from her feet then kicked his off as well before climbing onto the ultra-comfortable mattress topped with layers of soft covers and a mass of pillows.

"This thing feels like a cloud." His sigh fanned stray hairs from her forehead. "It's easy to believe I found an angel tonight."

"I don't plan to be that wholesome." Another laugh mingled with their desire as she reached up to bite his bottom lip.

Chase levered himself onto straight-locked arms to peer into her eyes. "Really? How do you want this to go? Slow and gentle aren't my specialties, but you make me want to take the scenic route and enjoy every curve of your gorgeous body."

"I could work with that." Preparing herself for the torture of an extended teasing, she realized he'd only paused—not finished—when he offered another option.

"Then again, if you'd rather something a little more daring… Well, I know you must have been craving at least something slightly out of the ordinary if you ventured into Underground tonight."

She closed her eyes and moaned as she imagined him peppering her with kisses in an endless midnight seduction.

Until the fantasy morphed into one where he took her harder. Faster. With the inherent authority she'd desperately tried to surrender tonight. Maybe he would even lay his palm on her ass as he took her from behind, giving her more than she could have dreamed possible at the beginning of the night.

Though both scenarios appealed—like two amazing dessert options on a menu—she knew which flavor she hungered for tonight.

If Linley said *I confess, I'm a hopeless romantic,* turn to page 124, *Romantic Interlude.*

If Linley said *Let's be nice and naughty,* turn to page 69, *A Pinch Of Spice.*

Stay Downstairs

Linley smirked. "Go home? I don't think so. Not until I've had a taste of this place—and you."

"Ah, that's what I figured. You don't strike me as a quitter." He kissed her quick and hard. "I like to be right, though."

She took a step toward the curtain, surprised when his fingers wrapped around her wrist to stall her. "Don't tell me you changed *your* mind?"

"Not going to happen, love." The grin lighting up his handsome face mesmerized her. "But you're a bit overdressed for Downstairs."

When he lifted his chin in the direction of the shadowed corner, she realized an attendant monitored a bank of lockers. "We'll leave our clothes here. You can keep your underwear if you prefer, but most patrons go bare beyond this point. I'm surely not going to complain if you decide to jump right in."

As he spoke, he unknotted the light blue silk tie he wore. Loosening the material from around his neck, he got to work on the buttons of his crisp shirt. Frozen, she stared as he put himself on display for her. Tan skin took the place of his fancy clothes. Naked looked so much better on him than his designer suit that she nearly swallowed her tongue.

"Thank you." His smug smile had her shaking her head, tempted to pinch the disc of his nipple, which tightened at the loss of his shirt.

Deciding it'd be better to undress before he had nothing left to occupy his attention and could stare at her in return, she curled her fingers in the hem of her dress. Several deep breaths later, she walked the pliant material up her thighs.

Chase groaned. "You're gorgeous. I'm a sucker for long,

pretty legs."

"Who wouldn't love those?" The attendant winked at her.

"Focus on me." Her escort drew her gaze to him once more. "There will be lots of people and distractions around tonight. If you get shy or overwhelmed, concentrate on me and ignore the rest."

Either her imagination played tricks or he'd edged closer when she glanced away from him. His suit jacket, tie, and shirt were draped over his forearm. He extended them toward the attendant then got to work on his belt. The *clink* of the buckle coming free, then the leather slipping through his loops, had her shivering. She watched as he toed off his shoes.

"Don't worry. It's warmer inside. The floor has radiant heat as well." Chase paused to rub his hand along her arm. "The sooner you strip, the sooner I can show you."

Linley bit her lip. She peeled the dress over her hips, up her stomach, and above her breasts. Ducking out of the outfit, she handed it to the attendant. One hand propped on her hip, she stood before Chase in heels and lacy black lingerie.

"I shouldn't have looked until I finished getting this damn zipper open." He cursed mildly beneath his breath, inciting a riot of giggles from her.

"Need some help?" She reached for him and he relented, allowing her to tuck her fingers in the waistband of his pants.

"Pretty sure that's only going to make the problem worse," he grumbled.

Bold and unafraid, Linley rubbed her palm over the bulge impeding his progress. She measured his length with her curious fingers then shifted the pressure from his zipper.

"Was that a purr you just made?" He grunted as he finally worked his trousers open.

"Might have been." Unable to stop herself, she leaned in for a kiss. The press of his smooth chest on her mostly unclothed skin had her breath catching in her lungs. While their mouths teased each other, he dropped his pants.

"Excuse me, Chase." The attendant cleared his throat. "I'm going to have to ask you kids to take this into Downstairs. You know the rules."

"Sorry, Nick." Chase broke their lip lock to apologize. He scrubbed his knuckles over his eyes and breathed deep as if trying to get himself under control.

The racing of her heartbeat meant she could relate. Nice to know she wasn't the only one revved to the max. To speed along the process, Linley sank to her knees at his feet. He glanced down at her then scrunched his eyes closed. "You can't do that here, love."

"What? Take your pants off?" She nipped the bulge of his quad as she tapped one of his heels. "Lift for me."

When he did, she swept his pants—and the gray boxer briefs he'd also shimmied down to his ankles—from his foot. Shortly, they repeated the gesture on his other side. She gained her feet carefully, thankful for his hands beneath her arms, helping her rise. Especially when she got an up close and personal view of his thick hard-on.

Tonight was going to be one for the history books, she was sure.

She handed her clothes to the attendant, who beamed at her. "I wish I wasn't on duty the whole evening. I've never seen our boy so dazzled before. This could be fun to watch."

Linley gasped. "Is this a spectator sport?"

"Only if that's what you want." Chase addressed her uncertainty in a flash. "Tonight is about your pleasure. You tell me what you'd like to try and I'll make it happen. Or prevent you from being exposed to something that isn't a turn on for you."

This time he folded his frame, crouching to slip her shoes from her feet one by one. "These are sexy as hell, but you don't need them."

This time when they stood facing each other, Chase dwarfed Linley. Or it seemed that way to her since it wasn't very often a man had several inches on her nearly six foot frame.

"It's a rare treat to be with a woman close to my height." He appraised her figure. At least her time in the gym had been well spent despite her busy schedule. It made her proud of her figure when he paused to admire the swell of her breasts and the dip of her waist. "You're svelte. Yet stacked."

"What are you going to do about it?" Linley shifted, trying to appease the pressure between her legs. Letting her gaze roam over the cut lines of his chest and abdomen, she couldn't wait for the instant he joined them together in this mutual desire.

"I'm going to show you a good time." He rose, passing her shoes to Nick.

"Have fun you two." The guy waved to them as Chase rested his palm at the small of her back and steered her toward the curtain.

"No doubt about that," he whispered, leaning in to nuzzle the soft fall of her hair at her temple. "Ready?"

"I'm standing here in my underwear, aren't I?" She angled her head to soften her joke with a quick kiss on his cheek.

"Quite beautifully, yes." The tip of his finger trailed along the edge of one of her bra cups. "I'm sort of glad you left the good stuff for me alone. Do you mind *me* being naked?"

"Hell no." A laugh bubbled out of her. He had the ability to put her at ease, even in a potentially awkward situation. "You were meant to be like this. For you, wearing clothes should be a crime."

"Likewise, Linley." After leaning in, he forced himself to stop. "Come on, let's go inside before I forget myself and break a rule or twenty. You know, that's not usually a problem for me."

"Thank you." She smiled up into his bewildered face, then latched on to his hand and dragged him through the curtain into Downstairs.

The moment she set foot on the warm floor, heat burst through her. Her eyes opened wide as she took in the debauchery around her. Each place her stare landed, a new experience unfolded. From the nude servers, passing out drinks, to the couples mingling as though they hung around associates in the buff every day—hell, maybe they did.

In awe, she didn't realize at first that some of the couples in the corners were doing more than simply socializing. Several of them were having sex, right there in the open. Others teased in foreplay intended to stimulate both the exhibitionists and their complimentary voyeurs stationed around the room.

A couple came through the curtain and bumped into her and Chase. "Come on, love. Let's take a closer look. And while we're touring, don't forget to peek at the doors to your right. Their names tell you a lot about what's waiting inside. If something looks interesting, let me know."

Overwhelmed with carnal delights, Linley allowed her guide to shuffle them forward. Several members admired his fresh find openly. He greeted some, waved to others across the room, and never once took his attention from her, monitoring her expression to all that surrounded them.

He headed for the back of the long, narrow space past endless couches on the left and a parade of ornate wooden doors with plaques. The very first one piqued her interest off the bat. It read: The Toy Chest.

They continued on past Peeping Toms, Vanilla, The Grotto, and Costumes 'R Us. Each had a vacant or occupied light illuminated on the front. They went on for as far as she could see until the portals turned a corner. She didn't doubt as many or more lurked around the edge. One in particular had her shivering, and not out of fear or disgust either.

Ties That Bind.

She hummed.

"You like that idea, huh?" Chase brushed his free thumb across the hard tip of her nipple, which distorted the front of her bra.

"Yes," she murmured. "It's all your fault. Since you showed me that painting in the hall, it's been on my mind."

"So noted." A chuckle emanated from his chest. "Why don't we take a seat for a while so you can check out the crowd and think about your choices? There are more around the bend if none of those appealed."

"No, I saw a few..." She had to clear her throat.

"Good." Chase squeezed her hand. "But I don't think you're fired up enough yet. I want you begging."

"That can be arranged." Stifling a pout became surprisingly difficult. Linley hardly recognized the woman he made her. Pliant. Needy. Vulnerable.

It frightened her and thrilled her at the same time.

"I'm talking about the kind of urge that burns until you scream my name and implore me to fill you. I'll make you want it all then give you more than you imagined." He certainly knew how to push her buttons. "Just like Alec is doing for Eliana."

"Hmm?" She glanced away from his handsome face toward whatever had snagged his attention.

A platinum blonde woman with extra-pale skin and a smattering of colorful tattoos was splayed on her back on a padded bench. A thin man boasting at least a dozen piercings, which reflected glints of his spiky blue hair, crawled between long, toned legs.

Whoa. "They're beautiful together," she whispered.

"I agree." Chase led her to a loveseat and pressed her shoulders until she lowered herself into the soft leather. "And she loves to have an audience to witness what her husband has the power to do to her."

"They're married?" Linley didn't object when Chase petted her long tresses where they spilled over her back nearly to her elbows. She reveled in the stoking touches. Accompanied by the sight of the fit, young couple in front of her—and the sounds of their lovemaking—she felt the warmth that had begun to pulse through her core growing. Spreading.

"Yes." He added kisses and licks to her neck and shoulders before toying with the upper swells of her breasts. "They met here and tied the knot within a few weeks. Right upstairs in the ballroom. At the time I thought they were crazy, but they've lasted. Must be coming up on five years now. And maybe I finally understand more about how they knew so fast. I've never felt this kind of chemistry before, Linley."

She pried her stare from Alec, who feasted on his wife as if he could never have enough of her taste. Eliana's spine arched as she offered herself more fully to the man she'd pledged herself to for life. Their demonstration was proof of their love and lust.

Alec pressed his wife's thighs wider apart to make room for his broad shoulders as he nestled closer to her core. She obliged, allowing him to mold her into whatever contortion he needed to improve his access.

"Wait, are you saying…" Afraid to ask, Linley knew tonight had already come to mean more to her than a quick let off of steam.

"Shh." Chase tipped her chin up and toward him so that he could claim her mouth. His kiss melted her doubts, leaving only searing desire. His tongue teased the insides of her lips then coaxed her own out to play. They swirled the wet muscles around each other, pausing only to suck or impart a love bite on the other. "I don't know what the hell is happening. But I'm going with it. I'm prepared to ride this wave as far as we can."

His hand wandered from her shoulder to cup her breast, testing the weight in his palm. She made a handful plus some for him, and he seemed plenty satisfied with the way they fit. Soon she wished the thin, expensive lace of her bra didn't stand between them making skin-to-skin contact.

"Chase," she whimpered.

"Almost." His denial strained, hopefully with similar need.

Linley allowed her hand to wander from where it'd hung limp by her side when he attacked her logic. She swept it over his muscled thigh until she bumped into the heaviness of his erection. Her fingers curled around the thick shaft possessively.

Chase broke their kiss as he practically growled her name. Triumph rang through her at the matching desperation in his stare. Instead of caving to her manipulation, he counterstriked. His fingers journeyed along her belly to cup her mound.

The mewl that broke from her throat surprised her.

Several of the couples around them diverted their attention from Alex and Eliana to the side action she and Chase were quickly ramping up to. If they didn't get behind closed doors soon, they'd be demonstrating more than she felt up to on her first time out.

Though she couldn't find her voice, she begged Chase with her gaze.

"Okay, I think we're ready." His self-deprecating laugh made it clear he wasn't used to suffering the same level of arousal as the women he delighted. Before she realized what he intended, he'd hailed a server. "When Robbie gets here, we'll give him our room order. Where am I taking you?"

"There are so many possibilities, it's hard to pick." Assaulted by a barrage of images, she closed her eyes. That only served to make the possibilities more vivid.

"You know, we can try them all eventually. But for tonight…why don't you tell me which two struck your fancy and we'll narrow it down from there." He patted her hand, lingering to tease the sensitive spots between her fingers, making her shiver.

"What if you don't like the activities on top of my list?" She gulped. Temptation loomed so near, she didn't relish the thought of being disappointed or putting him off.

"There aren't any doors in this room I wouldn't walk through with you." The wash of his breath proved he'd leaned in close enough to buss her cheek. "It's the reason I play up here instead of in the Basement. I know my limits and what I'm capable of granting a woman. Nothing here is out of the realm of enjoyment for me. So what are your top two?"

She opened her eyes and stared into the honest passion in his. "The Toy Chest and Ties That Bind."

"Damn." He tipped his head back and breathed hard. Had he gambled and lost?

"You don't approve?" She worried her lip. "I can choose something else."

"No, no." He pulled her onto his lap.

The throb of his cock against her belly had her gasping. "You like them both. A lot."

"Two of my favorites, love." The affirmation he growled against her neck preceded a nip and several kisses. "You were made for this. For me. For tonight."

She rubbed her breasts against his chest, counting on the solid muscles to soothe the ache through her bra.

"If we both like the options, how will we pick?" She tipped her head.

"Fate's been kind to us so far tonight." Chase kissed the corner of her mouth. "Whichever comes open first will be the one we go with. Fair?"

Linley nodded. She liked the idea of some randomness

to the fun. Either option filled her with longing and had her squirming on Chase's lap. Part of her needed him bad enough she considered adjusting their bodies the slight tilt it would take to have him inside her right here, the hell with anyone who saw.

Maybe that could be an adventure for another night. If…would he want to see her again? She hoped so but didn't plan to ruin the moment with long-term worries. That was the Ms. Lane she'd come here tonight to evade.

The server approached. Chase asked, "Is there a waiting list for Ties That Bind or The Toy Chest?"

Robbie shook his head. "You're in luck. Both are about to be available."

"We'll take whichever opens first." Chase informed the staffer.

"You got it, Chase." He smiled then wandered off to a serving station to punch the order into a computer.

Linley stared at the two doors behind them. Both rooms had the occupied light illuminated, though she could have sworn she'd seen a couple emerge a few minutes ago in the reflection from the huge gilt mirrors across the room. The scent and sounds of intense lovemaking surrounding them must be throwing off her senses.

"Both are empty." Chase read her thoughts. "They sanitize the play areas and reset them between couples. It should be any—"

He cut off as one of the lights flipped from red to green.

Linley's heart raced. She'd gotten her first choice after all.

"You've gone so stiff." He licked her collarbone. His hand dropped to her ass and kneaded the clenched muscles there. "Like you're about to come just thinking about what's in store for us. Jesus. You're amazing. Which one is it? The Toy Chest or Ties That Bind?"

If the open room is *Toy Chest,* turn to page 91, *Toy Chest With Chase.*

If the open room is *Ties That Bind,* turn to page 134, *Ties That Bind With Chase.*

Romantic Interlude

"When I set out tonight, I thought I'd have to do something daring to get what I needed. But now I realize it wouldn't have mattered. You're all I want. Relief from the stress of everyday and release from this tension that's been building." She smiled shyly into his gorgeous blue eyes. "Can we take it slow? No games. No crazy stuff. Just you and me. Enjoying each other."

"Of course," he murmured. "I'd have suggested it myself except disappointing you wasn't my intention. This feels right, Linley. I mean, we are sleeping together after having just met. That's wild enough, isn't it?"

"Insane. And somehow not." She reached up to stroke his cheek.

"Would you mind if I lit some of those candles?" The flick of his chin toward her mantle and the side tables helped her understand despite the fog in her brain.

"Of course not. Go ahead. There are matches in the dish beside the pillars." Linley watched as he stalked from cluster to cluster of the pretty votives, jars, and sticks. She adored candles of every variety.

Flame caught as soon as he touched the head to the striker. She could sympathize with the poor bit of tinder. He'd set her ablaze with as little effort. When he'd finished ringing them in the warm yellow glow of flickering light, he extinguished the overhead lamp and returned to their nest.

He rolled until they faced each other on their sides. Lounging in bed, they whispered as they kissed and caressed each other through their clothes. For how long, she couldn't say. Maybe hours. They joked. Discovered sensitive areas and practiced reducing their partner to sighs of delight.

When she couldn't stand it anymore, Linley got to her knees on the mattress.

"What are you doing, love?" Chase smiled up at her, his attentive stare following every move she made.

"Getting rid of some of these pesky barriers." She collected the hem of her dress in her fingers and began to draw it upward.

When Chase licked his lips, she teased him by lowering it once more.

"I'll be good, I promise." He winked up at her.

"Why don't I believe you?" A laugh fell from her parted lips as she wished she hadn't stopped kissing him. The skill with which he infused desire into his smallest movements had her longing to return to his embrace.

"Because you're smart." He chuckled along with her.

This time she lifted the material until all of her legs were on display. A tiny bit more and she'd reveal the black lace of her thong to his hungry gaze.

"Show me."

"Are you sure you want to see?" The longing in his eyes didn't lie. Something about him made her flirtatious side emerge.

She hadn't even known she had one before tonight.

"Positive." Chase lounged nearby, appraising her. His deceptive relaxation made her imagine a lion sunning itself, yet ready to explode into action at any given instant.

His fingers toyed with her knee and the bare skin just above it. Though he could outwait her, she didn't care about the contest of wills. It delighted her that he seemed content to drink in her display and humor her artless seduction.

Simple pleasures sustained them both.

Except she'd waited so long… She yearned for more.

Linley forced a deep breath past her flipping insides and the tight band of hope squeezing her in the vicinity of her heart. With her courage dialed up, she peeled her dress above her hips and paused with it ringing her mostly flat belly.

"A little faster, love." Chase hadn't blinked in a while. Perhaps his impatience was mounting too. He began to creep closer, stalking her from his prone position on her enormous bed.

She swallowed then whipped the stretchy fabric over her head and flung it into the corner where it draped over a wingback chair she loved curling up in to read. When time permitted, which hadn't been often enough. Tonight was one of the few things she'd done strictly for fun in a while.

Parts of her whispered that what she'd stumbled across was something more important than physical amusement, but she jammed the rational side of her back into the closet before the fuddy-duddy could spoil the entertainment for the evening.

"Wait," Chase rasped. "Stay just like that."

Linley froze with her hands up, tangled in her hair, where she'd been unconsciously finger combing the mussed strands. She met his intense stare. "Why?"

"Because I'm taking a mental picture." He groaned. "You're gorgeous. This place, the light, your bed—you. So soft, like a secret hideaway where a fair maiden is just waiting for me."

"I'm not exactly a virgin." She snorted. They both cracked up at her faux pas. Laughing in bed with him had to be one of the biggest turn-ons of all time. "Are you a knight in shining armor? Or maybe a prince?"

"Not exactly. If you'd wanted that option, you should have stuck with Ryder." He grimaced.

"What?" She canted her head.

"Shit. Sorry." Chase reached for her, and she tumbled willingly into his hold. "You're making me lose my mind. I shouldn't have said that. Club rules and all."

"Is he really…?" Linley attempted to put that mantle on the rough-and-tumble man yet couldn't manage it.

"Yeah. But you didn't hear that from me." Covering her mouth, he kept them from discussing the topic in any more detail. This time his hands roamed across her naked flesh. They were warm and gentle but not too soft. Quickly, all thoughts of other men fled her mind. They vanished from her bedroom. "That's better, love."

He gazed into her eyes as he traced the contour of her smile with one fingertip. "So, should I finish undressing you? Or would you like me to even the score?"

"That." Stealing her ability to speak intelligently, she selected from his menu of options. "The second one."

She couldn't wait to see him naked. The press of his firm planes through his clothes guaranteed the view would be spectacular.

Linley propped herself on the heap of pillows at the head of her bed and tucked her feet beneath her.

"Would you like some popcorn?" He chuckled though she had to make sure she wasn't drooling when he worked the knot of his tie loose. His long, thick fingers began to deftly tuck the buttons of his Oxford through the holes.

"Shh…" Linley played along. "Don't talk during the good parts."

"I didn't think I'd gotten there yet." He spread his shirt wide, treating her to a glimpse of his washboard abs.

"Oh yeah, I think that's going to be one of my favorite sections." Dying to run a single finger down the center of his gorgeous body, she clasped her hands in front of her to ensure she behaved.

"Hmm." His wry smile did funny things to her. "I hope there's at least one you like better."

With that he worked the buckle of his belt apart and slid the length of leather from around his trim waist. It hit the plush carpet with a dull thud. Practically before it sounded, he'd drawn his zipper down and separated the placket of his trousers.

Already she could see the silhouette of his arousal through the gray boxer briefs he wore beneath. "Okay. You win. I'm pretty fond of what you've got going on there."

Chase chuckled as he shucked the pants along with the open shirt. His underwear followed a moment later. The lithe flex of his body had her dreaming of a whole new level of pleasure he could drive her to tonight.

And that was before she allowed herself to check out the length of his erection, standing thick against his lightly-furred stomach.

Linley blinked. Then did it again.

"Thanks, love." He whipped one side of the covers back then lifted her and slid her beneath them. Cocooned, she didn't even squirm when he attacked her panties. His fingers tucked under the lace and peeled it from her. She lifted her ass, helping him divest her of the final obstruction between them.

Well, second to last really. But it only took him a few instants more to have her bra unhooked and falling from her arms. When the cups released her body, leaving her nipples to harden with the wash of room temperature air, she ducked her head.

With a man as fine as him…

"Never doubt how beautiful you are, Linley." Chase nudged her chin up until he could reclaim her lips.

He rubbed hers with his, transferring some of the dampness there. The intensity of his stare never abandoned her eyes while he massaged her tongue and gums. Simultaneously, he soothed her and aroused her. It shouldn't have been possible. But with him, almost anything seemed to be.

When he sank lower, his bare chest made contact with her breasts and his cock prodded her thigh. She arched, pressing closer, as tight to his heat and generous affection as she could get. Candlelight glinted off the bronze highlights in his hair. He looked like a god come to life.

Yet he seemed equally as enthralled by her.

Their lips drifted apart as he slowly retreated. Next he placed a kiss on the corner of her mouth, teasing her permanent smile. After he'd finished paying his respects to the joy they created in unison, he trailed his open mouth along her jaw, then beneath her ear.

A shiver rubbed her against the length of his body.

They both groaned.

That didn't impede his progress, however. He licked at her collarbone then the swells of her chest. Linley attempted to feed him her nipple but he danced around the edges, threatening to make her crazy with need.

Finally, his other hand cupped one of her breasts, plumping it as his mouth drew on the peak of the other. She gasped and threw her head back, her hair splaying on the pillow around her face.

It was a sight he must have appreciated when he glanced up because his cock throbbed against her thigh. Linley wrapped one leg around him, attempting to draw him inward.

"Not yet," he whispered.

"I think I changed my mind." She couldn't help it. Her nails pressed crescents into his powerful shoulders, loving the pads of muscle there, which absorbed the tiny pricks. "Maybe we should go fast after all."

"I don't think so." He clasped her nipple between his teeth and tugged ever so lightly. "Stay strong, love."

"Easy for you to say. You're out of reach." She pouted just a bit. "Let me put my mouth on you and see how you feel then."

"Not tonight." He shook his head. "This is about your pleasure. This is what you've picked. Enjoy what I can give you."

As if he sensed her limits were nearing, he ducked his head and kissed his way down the middle of her torso. When he reached her mound, he paused. The wash of his breath caressed her exposed flesh and highlighted the nerves beneath the damp area.

"You smell delicious." He nuzzled her, breathing deep.

His body spread her legs bit by bit until she splayed before him. Settling into the valley she made for him, he showed her just how well they fit together. Her thighs rested on his shoulders and his arms swept beneath them to support the arch of her back.

Comfortable and surprisingly not awkward, she relaxed into his hold. Good thing he had quite a grip, because the instant his mouth settled on her pussy, she bucked. It would have been impossible to stay still at the rush of sensation he imparted.

Sure, guys had gone down on her before. Never with the finesse and attention he devoted to the exploration led by his tongue, backed up by the rest of his mouth. Chase applied suction over her clit, making her whimper and swing her hips in an arc designed to feed him every ounce of the juices coating her.

Each lap of his tongue encouraged more to spill from within and onto his chin. He didn't seem to mind. If anything, the unmistakable confirmation of their chemistry spurred him on. Before she could beg for more, he granted her the addition of his finger.

He slid one digit deep inside her with hardly any effort.

Still she hugged it tight, the walls of her pussy undulating around the invasion in time to the manipulation of his tongue, which now flicked over and across her clit.

Linley's eyes rolled back in her head. Her mouth hung open to emit the steady cries he inspired. Her fingers speared into his hair, holding him exactly where she needed his attention most.

She wanted to warn him that he teased her too much. Nothing would work right, or maybe sex before had never been so good it disengaged the link between her brain and mouth. His name tore from her throat as she lifted her head to look at him directly.

Chase glanced at her long enough to take stock and wink. Then he delved deeper into her folds. Resisting would have been impossible. The shimmering pleasure coalesced. It turned random spasms into a pattern of delightful clenches that built toward an orgasm.

Gentle rubbing of his finger from the inside paired with his skilled nibbling on the outside to send her pussy into convulsions.

Linley's heels drummed on his back as she shattered.

She came so hard she could have sworn the candles floated in her vision. Meanwhile, Chase's praise blanketed her as did his comforting kisses and featherweight touches.

Despite all his efforts, nothing quieted the desire raging inside her. Temporary relief wouldn't be enough to quench the fire they'd lit tonight. When he kissed her softly then pulled away to smile, she whispered, "I want you."

"Give it a minute." He settled in beside her, cradling her. "There's no hurry. I'm not leaving unless you'd prefer—"

"No!" She tempered her denial, toning it down just a tad. "I wouldn't like that at all. And I think I've waited long enough to have you."

Linley knew he'd understand she meant far more than the brief time they'd spent in anticipation tonight. She couldn't believe she'd gone her whole life without the intimacy of this connection. Sex with Chase made her previous lovers seem like a joke. A ghost of what might be.

So when he rolled out of her arms, she tried to grab him. It wasn't her proudest moment. She didn't give a damn.

"I'm not going far," he promised as he lunged for the side of the bed. "Just to get a condom from my wallet."

"Oh." She blushed. "Right then."

As simply as that, their laughter returned, even in the

face of searing heat and potential awkwardness. He smiled as he teased her. "Nice to know I'm wanted though."

Linley licked her lips as he ripped open the foil packet and rolled the thin latex over the length of his erection. It seemed even bigger now than it had on first glimpse. Tentatively, she reached out. He moaned when her fingers curled around him then stroked from root to tip a few times.

"Is that what you want, love?" He gulped, causing his Adam's apple to bob.

"Yes."

"You're sure." He turned serious for an instant. "I don't want to risk what's developing between us on a night of fantastic sex. If you're going to wake up tomorrow and freak out... Well, I'd rather we fall asleep together instead."

"You seriously think you're going to drift off with that thing begging for attention?" She pointed at his cock.

He laughed again. "Uh, not for a while. Or maybe with a trip to the bathroom for some solo action. But I'm willing to try. I'm not kidding around, Linley."

"I'm not going to regret this. Not in the morning. Or ever." She leaned over to kiss him softly. "I'm only going to be unhappy if we *don't* go ahead. There's nothing to debate. It's the easiest decision I've ever made. You make it a no-brainer."

With a growl, he rose over her. In a flash, he had her pinned beneath him. The tip of his cock was poised to tunnel inside her body.

Instead of waiting for him to make the decision, she chose to lift, initiating penetration.

The instant they were joined, even the barest bit, she swore her whole world tilted on its axis. Chase squeezed his eyes shut for a moment. When he opened them, she swore the hint of a sheen lingered on top of the bright blue that reminded her of a summer sky or the ocean in the tropics.

"I promise this will be better next time," he rasped.

"I don't see how it could be." Linley moaned as he advanced, stretching her to accommodate his girth.

"Well it might last more than twenty-seven fucking seconds." He gritted his teeth.

"Yes, they will be *fucking* seconds, won't they?" She adored his grin and the way it mixed with smoky satisfaction.

"Uh huh." He glided inside her until he bottomed out. Then retreated until he nearly slipped from her grip. "One."

Never before had she laughed and had sex at the same time. Nothing had ever felt as good.

Their ridiculousness faded when his mouth came down on hers in a scorching kiss punctuated by the grind of their pelvises and the plunging of his thick cock. The things he did to her, inside and out, transported her to another time and place where only they existed. The ecstasy they gifted each other was the only thing that mattered.

And when cords began to stand out on Chase's neck, her body responded. Clenching around him—tightening, quickening—she matched his escalation step by step, until they'd climbed to the pinnacle together.

He stared into her eyes. The brilliance of the emotion there shoved her over the edge.

Together, they jumped. Soared.

"Linley!" He called her name as he held her tight, protected her from anything outside the sphere of light and heat they generated while he poured himself into her.

And when they'd finished quaking beneath the force of their connection, they fell still, bonded together by the shared experience.

To find out what happened next, turn to page 161, *Chase Epilogue*.

Ties That Bind With Chase

"Ties That Bind is open," Linley whispered. A shiver ran through her.

"Hell, yes." The pressure of Chase's fingers on her cheek tipped her face toward him. He stole a deep kiss. He ended the sweet yet dirty meeting of their mouths prematurely. "Come on, before someone beats us to it."

They practically hurdled the couch in their haste to abscond to the fantasy chamber. When they drew up short in front of the elaborately carved hardwood, Chase paused with his hand on the knob.

"No second guessing here." She answered before he could ask. "Let's do this. Show me what's behind that door."

"You got it." He laughed at her eagerness. Not in a mean way, but with an indulgent partner-in-crime sort of flavor.

They held hands as he pushed the panel open and drew her inside, closing them in darkness together. When he slid the dimmer up gradually, she gasped.

The room was the stuff of erotic daydreams. Gold accents offset the forest green walls. Enormous gilded mirrors reflected her stunned expression and Chase's undivided focus on her reaction.

He smiled as she discovered the nuances of the space.

Silk scarves in every hue draped along one of the walls. The waterfall of colors and softness took her breath away. Linley wandered to the display. A board with infinite hooks, like an extended horizontal coat rack, ran along the full length of the room above the height of her head. Extravagant material hung from each.

A rainbow of dirty intentions shimmered beneath her fingers as she dragged them through the luxurious fabric.

They rippled in the wake of the air she disturbed as she passed.

"They're beautiful. It's like a painting. Or a tapestry, I guess." Entranced, she allowed one to run through her fingers.

"Stunning and functional." Chase approached behind her. He rested his hands on her hips and snugged her back to his chest. The heat radiating from his body permeated her awe. "What's your favorite color?"

"Blue," she replied.

"I'm not surprised. It's mine also." He guided her to that part of the spectrum then selected several scarves in a variety of shades—ice, sky, sapphire, cornflower, and one that reminded her of the cerulean water that lapped the shoreline in the backyard of her Bonaire vacation home.

"Um, Chase..." She hated to seem so ignorant.

"Changing your mind?" The idea didn't seem to upset him. He'd shape their night into a pleasurable experience no matter what, she was sure of it.

"Not at all." Linley spun in his arms, coming to face him so that he could read the honesty in her expression. "Just wondering why you need five. Last time I checked, I only had four limbs."

A glimpse of his smoldering smile made her embarrassment worthwhile. "One's to cover your eyes."

"Oh." She closed them and considered what it would be like to have him touch her when all she could focus on was the sound of him stalking her along with the feel of his seduction. Her eyes popped open. "I think I like the idea of that."

"I'm glad." He leaned in and laid his lips on hers. They kissed long and slow before he broke away to allow them to draw in a much-needed breath. "I'm going to have so much fun with you. Just wait until you're stretched out, every inch of you bared to me, and there's nothing you can do but accept the pleasure I give you."

Linley whimpered. "I'm not so good at being passive."

"Maybe not usually. I can see that." He tucked an errant wave of hair behind her ear. "But tonight is different. You came here because normal wasn't working for you, didn't you?"

Of course he was right. She nodded.

"Then trust me to know what you need." Chase gestured around the room to the variety of ornate lacquered chests and wardrobes they hadn't explored yet. "There are plenty of other options contained in these four walls. But something tells me this is exactly what you need."

"I believe you."

"Plus, it gives you a reason to come back with me some other time." He bumped his fist on the top of one of the storage units they passed. "We'll delve into more elaborate options in the future. For tonight, simple is best."

"You've given me plenty of excuses to seek you out again. If that's an option." She peeked at him as he led her to the enormous bed, the centerpiece of the rear wall.

"Hey, don't worry about anything other than the here and now." He ran his thumb over her fingers. "We'll figure out the rest later. Only pleasure is allowed within this room. Deal?"

"Yeah." Linley murmured against his lips an instant before he sealed them over hers once more.

He had an amazing ability to steal her doubt and transform it into something wonderful. What would it be like to have that in her life all the time? Given the pressure of her career and the real need for relaxation, a partner like him would be invaluable.

She sank into the play of his tongue over her gums and her own tensed muscle, which flicked at his in return. Eventually she found herself sucking lightly on his bottom lip. The rasp of her teeth across the damp flesh coaxed a moan from his sheltering chest. It was then she realized his fingers had slid up her spine and were deftly unhooking her bra.

A brush of silk on her back promised he hadn't abandoned the scarves in his hand to undress her. Linley insinuated a tiny gap between them. Just enough space to whisper, "Thank you for not tearing that. It's one of my favorites, from my last trip to Paris."

"I'm more of a savor-the-moment kind of guy. I unwrap all my presents nice and slow." He grinned. "Besides, I love the way this looks on you. Sexy as hell, love. You'll have to give me the name of the shop so I can browse there the next time I'm in the city."

She had to bite her cheek to keep from suggesting they visit together. After all, she had meetings with one of their international distribution partners there in two weeks.

"Thank you." A return trip to the boutique became a priority on her list of sightseeing activities.

Chase nudged the straps from her shoulders and the garment fell away, exposing her breasts to his ravenous stare. "But as lovely as it was, you—naked—is a million times better. Gorgeous."

He cupped her breasts, plumping them until they spilled over the top of his palms. Pressure built as he bent to kiss the mounds and draw lightly on each nipple.

Linley buried her fingers in his hair. At the contact of her massage on his scalp, he paused, shaking his head. "Ah, you make me forget my intentions. Why are those hands still free?"

"Hmm... Not sure. You're the one running this show." She giggled when he scooped her up and tossed her onto the super-sized bed. The cushy strata of duvets absorbed the impact of her body and had her snuggling into their plush depths.

Propped up on the bank of pillows, in assorted silk cases,

she had a perfect view of Chase leaping onto the bed and crawling between her legs with the scarves clutched between his teeth. He stalked her, his muscles rippling in the diffuse light cast by the half-bright wall sconces.

Instinctively, she spread her legs wider, granting him access to the only barrier left between them. He pounced, lunging forward until his fingers tucked into the waistband of the matching black panties of her lace set.

"Definitely geniuses." His praise took her a second to translate between his sexy mouthful and the haze of arousal fogging her mind. He must have noticed her confusion because he tipped his head to the side and dropped the scarves. They fluttered to the mattress in a swirl of blue shades.

Free of distractions, Chase trained his attention on her panties.

True to his word, he peeled the scrap from her a teeny bit at a time.

Finally, the underwear slid from her hips, down her thighs. She lifted her feet so he could take them off. After he tossed them on the floor beside her bra, she lowered her heels on either side of him once more. A wash of warm air puffed over her waxed mound. He observed her up close and personal, as if he were an art connoisseur studying the brush strokes of a painting for a rave review. Surprisingly, his scrutiny didn't embarrass her. Instead it made her feel beautiful, worthy of his attention.

Chase placed a kiss on her mound, just above her clit. "Hold that thought, love. I'll be back in a few seconds. As soon as I take care of some business."

She wondered what he meant until he rolled across the expansive bed toward a side table as if he were a commando invading enemy territory. He opened a drawer there and withdrew several condoms and a long, thin black box before returning to her side in an equal hurry.

The smile she hadn't lost all night remained firmly in place. He might act suave, but he needed her as fiercely as she craved him. Miraculous yet true. The connection between them had been instant and intense.

Still, it allowed room for curiosity and expanding her horizons.

Linley scrunched her pink-painted toes in the bedcovers when he stared at her like *that*.

"Would you like to see one of my favorite parts of this room?" He smiled.

"I think I'm looking at the best thing in here already," she murmured huskily.

Chase glanced down at his rock-hard cock. "You are having a profound effect on me."

She laughed. "That's not what I meant, and you know it. But now that you've mentioned it, he's not too shabby either. So how much longer are you going to tease me before taking me for a ride?"

"I'm afraid I can't draw this out as long as I would like." He frowned. "I usually have more self-control than this. But...you're getting under my skin, love."

"Glad to know the feeling's mutual." She reached for him but he dodged.

"Not just yet or I'll lose my mind before I give you what you've asked for." He shook his head, standing his ground. "I get the feeling you don't make requests like this often. I'm going to deliver."

"Really, Chase, you're enough. This thing between us, it's more than I'd hoped for." She held her arms up and open to him.

He took the opportunity to snag her wrists and hold them high above her, as far as she could comfortably reach. "Shush. Just watch...while you can."

Trembling—not from cold or fear—she gaped when he activated a button on the black box he still held in his free hand. It was a remote of some sort. The subtle whir of motors followed. Thin wires descended from discrete panels in the elaborate canopy above the bed. No wonder it was so ornate.

At the end of each dangled a ring. She didn't have to wonder about their purpose for long. Chase snagged one of the silk scarves from the bed then threaded it through the circle. With deft movements of his long, skilled fingers, he tied the material to the fastener. It made sense when she thought it through.

A bed this large wouldn't have accommodated even the generous lengths of the scarves. The equipment probably also allowed for more adventurous play. Maybe even suspension. She'd seen pictures on the Internet that made her moan just at the thought. Next time…

Once satisfied with the security of the silk, Chase slid his hand down the length then wrapped the other end around one of her wrists. He spread the fabric so that it became a wide cuff, which didn't cut into her skin in the least. Careful, he didn't fool around while he secured her then checked his handiwork.

"You're to tell me if you feel any numbness. Right away. Understand?" His serious tone brooked no argument.

"Agreed." She nodded.

"Damn it turns me on when you go all prim and proper." He stroked his erection a few times before reaching for another tie. "I can't wait to make you crack and turn dirty girl instead."

"Somehow I don't think that'll take long." She turned her head and nipped his ankle, which rested beside her as he treated her other wrist to similar treatment as the first.

And when he'd finished, he crouched beside her. Impressive balance kept him from squashing her on the flexible surface of the bed. "Let's see how good I did, shall we?"

The arrogant smirk on his face might have taunted a

smartass remark from her except that he chose that instant to slide his fingers over her belly to tickle her ribs. Linley thrashed. Her bindings held.

When she laughed so hard she could barely breathe, he relented. "Had to be sure you wouldn't hurt yourself if we get carried away."

He stood again to slide a finger beneath the improvised cuffs she wore like a fantastic accessory. Satisfied, he knelt down and kissed her.

Although she hadn't once considered retreating, having no choice in the matter made the gentle assault of his mouth that much more enjoyable. Her pussy quivered, and she arched toward him, her body begging for more.

"Almost," he whispered before departing again.

Chase poked a different button on the remote. Panels in the bar spanning the foot of the bed popped open. From them he withdrew two identical lines with twin metal hoops. He made quick work of mimicking her wrist fastenings on her ankles.

Spread wide—though not uncomfortably so—Linley groaned at the light pressure of the tensioned cables on her legs. Chase's quality control testing was distinctly more pleasurable.

He dropped into the *V* made by her thighs and snuggled up to the trunk of her body. She had to admit, his shoulders fit nicely there. Air stuck in her lungs when he extended his tongue and licked one long line from the bottom of her slit to her clit, pausing to circle the entrance of her pussy along the way.

Pure ecstasy rolled through her. When he pulled away, reaching for the last tie, she attempted to wrap her legs around his waist to prevent his retreat. No could do.

"Ah, perfect." He bent to lay a kiss on her nose. "Now, you'll have some idea of what it looks like so your imagination can fill in the blanks when you're blind and I do this."

Linley regretted she wouldn't witness his complete dismantling of her inhibitions. At least until the slippery material settled over her eyes and her personal dusk descended. The loss of her vision forced her to rely on her other senses, which magnified their input.

"You're doing great, love." Chase petted her, dissolving the last of her unease.

Unable to see him approach, the wet warmth of his mouth brushing hers came as a delightful surprise. She moaned and arched into the contact as best she could. Pleasant tugs on her wrists and ankles reminded her that she'd surrendered control. The pleasure storming her system renewed her faith in others.

Chase especially.

He would take care of her. When was the last time someone could say that?

A string of sighs left her mouth, each one in response to a kiss he placed on her body. The direction of their occurrence convinced her of his destination. She wished he'd hurry. But he didn't. And when he dallied at her hipbone, she nearly screamed.

Until he finally, finally settled his lips over her pussy.

Then she did shout. His name, some demands, God knew what else. But it didn't matter. There wasn't a single thing she could do to speed up the relentless cycle of licks and kisses he treated her to. If she hadn't been at his mercy, she might have given in to the guilt of their one-sided exchange, reaching for him to return the favor. But like this…she couldn't deny the treatment was his decision.

When he slipped a finger—then two—inside her, she knew there was one thing he couldn't regulate. Or didn't seem to want to. The inevitable pulses of her approaching orgasm began deep inside her belly. Before she could warn him of the effect he had on her, Chase groaned.

He broke contact, setting her adrift in blackness, for just long enough to encourage her. "You're so damn tight. Slick. More every second. You're close, aren't you?" Linley cried out her agreement.

"Then why are you holding back?" He nipped her thigh, startling a yelp from her.

And when she relaxed, the pleasure his hand delivered by working within her was more obvious than it had been before. Sensations bombarded her. All of them focused between her legs, where he touched her.

She had to be honest. "I want to come with you inside me."

"You will." He granted her wish. "But after you show me exactly how good it's going to be. Hug my hand. Come around me, love. I'll bring you with me again in a minute. Hurry, please. I need to bury myself in this soft heat soon."

His words contributed as equally to her destruction as his persuasive suckling did when his mouth latched on to her once more. His generosity mixed with the wicked things his tongue did to her clit. The circles he rubbed on her from the inside pushed her over the edge.

The pressure of her bindings as she contracted all over added to the swell of rapture in her. And suddenly it was all too much. She exploded, committing herself to enjoying every ounce of pleasure resulting from the epic orgasm he inspired.

Before she'd finished quaking, the rustle of foil ripping traveled to her overly alert ears.

An aftershock rocked her as she considered what was to come.

The spasm made it impossible for Chase to penetrate when he lined up the blunt head of his cock with her opening in the same instant. "I can't wait to feel you milking me like that."

His voice had changed. Gravelly, a little harsh, she knew

he was on the edge. She regretted that she wouldn't be able to recover quick enough to have her wish after all. But the beautiful release still singing through her veins made it impossible to be sad after the gift he'd given her.

He deserved to take.

"Fuck me, Chase." The dirty words slipped right out of her mouth. The blindfold might have helped. She felt free to say and do whatever she wanted, emancipated by the tools he'd used on her to their greatest advantage.

"Yes." He advanced with a powerful thrust that lodged him an inch or two deep in her still pulsing tissue. "There's the girl I was looking for. No more façade, Linley. I want the real woman. The one hiding inside."

He had no idea the mischief he'd unlocked.

"Give me your cock." She grunted when he retreated a bit then did as she demanded. Though she clearly had no authority, she felt as if he'd given her the power. To do as she'd dreamed forever without fear or self-doubt.

"More," she yelled.

He obeyed. A few more thrusts and they locked together as tightly as two people could get. The heat and pressure of his chest covered hers, relieving the aches in her breasts with the contact. His mouth covered hers and they kissed ferociously as he began to ride her.

The thick, long length of his cock filled her to capacity. Maybe a bit beyond. The burn only added to her desire. She'd never been stretched like this before. Not physically, or emotionally.

To her surprise, the killer climax she'd relished began to rejuvenate with the measured strokes he continued to supply between her legs. As they made out, he lost a little of his finesse and gained a bit of rawness that she savored.

"You're going to come with me, love." It wasn't a question. It was a command. The urgency with which he made it implied haste.

When she feared she might disappoint him, he added a swing of his pelvis to each lunge, grinding their bodies where they joined. The stimulation on her clit combined with his penetration, the weight of his body, which she supported gladly, and the sweetness of his kiss, invigorating every sensitive place inside her.

Tendrils of pure bliss rose within her. She focused on them, growing them until she shouted. "Now, Chase. I'm there. Coming."

"I know. Damn, love. I know." He grunted the last as her body began to squeeze him, making him work to tunnel as deep as he had been.

Chase didn't seem to mind. He fucked harder, faster, obeying the draw of her pussy. She screamed his name and was surprised to hear her own flying from his lips. In the midst of it all, he yanked the blindfold from her head. The sight of his handsome face, contorted in ecstasy, flung her even higher.

He pumped into her, making her wish she could feel each warm blast of his come, which she echoed with a wring of her pussy.

It went on and on until neither of them had the strength to move, or even moan.

Long, luxurious minutes passed where they absorbed the pleasure they'd created together until she kept her promise. "Chase."

"Yes, love?" He kissed her cheek with tenderness that threatened to bring tears to her eyes.

"My left hand is getting tingly." She wished they never had to move. "Sorry."

"Thank you for saying something. It's important for me to trust you if we're going to play like this…or more." He smiled at her as he released her then massaged her offended palm. "Go ahead, put your arms around me."

She didn't have to be told twice.

Linley snuggled up to his chest, laid her head on his shoulder, and hugged him tight.

To find out what happened next, turn to page 161, *Chase Epilogue.*

Ryder Epilogue

When the storm had passed, they lay wrecked on the bed. Silk sheets tangled around them, partially caught between their bodies, which pressed together everywhere else.

Please, please don't let real life ruin this.

Linley cleared her throat.

"Ryder, there's something I need to tell you." She bit her lip. Pressure built in her stomach as she considered the ramifications of coming clean. But this night had meant something to her. She couldn't ignore that. Linley refused to jeopardize their future by not being straight with him upfront. Mostly upfront.

"What's wrong?" He leaned on his elbow, brushing the hair from her face.

"I'm sort of...rich."

He laughed. "That's it? Wildcat, you're well off I'm sure, but so am I."

Linley didn't mean to crush his pride. "Actually, I'm the founder and owner of Lane Technology."

"I know, *Linley*. It's a beautiful and unique name. Like you. There can't be many of those around. Especially not women Henry would vouch for." He held her in place when she would have bolted. Betrayed, her stomach fell through the floor.

"You knew who I was?" She tried to block the tears of frustration welling in her eyes. It *had* been too good to be true. "The whole night?"

"Of course. I'm *not* a moron." He tried to subdue her with a kiss. For a few seconds it worked. And then he shocked her into total stillness. "But I *am* a prince. Go ahead, make your frog jokes here."

She gaped at him. "You mean like...*royalty?*"

"I know. No one else in my family can believe they had an heir as unsavory as me either." Ryder flopped an arm over his eyes. And that's when she noticed the family crest tattooed on the underside of his biceps. "Don't worry, I'll only make you kneel for me in the bedroom."

Bad boy sovereign. *Of course!*

She'd heard plenty of stories about him.

"Wow. It really is you, Prince Haider Naim."

"Yeah. If you say it fast, it almost sounds like Ryder, huh?" He grimaced. "At first it was an easy cover. Eventually it stuck."

"Are you sure sleeping with me won't ruin your image?" Linley wrung the edge of the sheet where it draped across her chest. "I've never been very scandalous before tonight."

"Look, if you wanted another squeaky clean captain of industry like yourself, you should have picked Chase. You know, Chase *Worthington.*" Count on Ryder to throw rules out the window. The breach also exposed his vulnerability.

Too many newsflashes bombarded her logic.

"Holy shit." She wondered if she'd heard right. "The venture capitalist?"

"Mmm hmm." Ryder patted her ass. "You didn't think Henry would throw you to the dogs, did you?"

"Well, no." Linley hadn't assumed anything at all. With such short notice, how had her friend uncovered two prime specimens for her to pick from?

"Underground is an escape for the ultra-elite, wildcat." He seemed wary, as if she would hit on the million dollar question any instant. And then she did.

"Captains of industry... Heads of state... If Underground is that exclusive, how is my chief of security a member?" Linley squinted at Ryder.

"That's a question you're going to have to ask Henry

yourself." Ryder clammed up for once. "He's already going to try to kick my ass for bringing you to the dark side here. At least until I tell him it's not what he thinks."

"And what will he assume?" She bit her lip to keep from revealing too much of her own emotion.

"That I was just fucking around like I usually do." Her fallen prince looked like he needed a hug, so she obliged. He squeezed her tight in return. "Damn, you're sweet and honest and so fucking sexy you nearly melted parts of me. Actually, maybe you did."

Ryder rubbed his chest as if it ached.

She kissed him until some of his tension vanished.

"Thanks. But I'm dying to know…" He closed his eyes then asked, "Was this just some erotic adventure for you, or would you consider dating a guy like me despite all the bullshit drama that it will entail? Will you give us a chance? Yes or no?"

For Linley, there was only one option. "Yes."

The End

Ryder Loves The Toy Chest

"I requested a romp in the Toy Chest." Linley beamed when he grinned. A shiver ran through her.

"Fuck, yes." Ryder caught her off guard when he threw her over his shoulder and marched toward the fantasy chamber. He drew up short in front of the elaborately carved hardwood. When she peeked around his trim waist, she saw he paused with his hand on the knob.

"No second guessing here." She answered before he could ask. "Let's do this. Show me what's inside. I hope there's a bed, or a thick rug at least, because I need you to get me horizontal fast."

"What do you have against being fucked standing up? It can be plenty enjoyable." He grunted when she smacked his smoking-hot ass. "Fine, feisty. I'm going."

Ryder ducked inside, closing them in darkness together. He lowered her to the ground and spun her so she faced the interior with him at her back. When he slid the dimmer up gradually, she gasped.

The room was the stuff of erotic daydreams. Burnished silver accents offset the deep purple of the walls. A gorgeous oval mirror reflected her stunned expression and Ryder's undivided focus on her reaction.

He smiled as she discovered the nuances of the chamber.

Armoires and dressers lined each available space on the perimeter. They ringed a low, tufted bench, which stretched across the foot of an enormous four-poster bed complete with a draped silk canopy.

Silver and purple sheets were perfectly tucked and a whole host of pillows called to her, inviting her to crash into their fluffiness. Naked. With this exotic, sexy, roguish guy who seemed to be as enthralled by her as she was with him.

What more could she want?

Oh, right. Toys.

An enormous smile spread across her face.

"That's the spirit, wildcat." Ryder smacked her ass lightly as he drew her toward some of the dressers and began to undo several intricate latches. He flipped up lids, opened cabinets, and drew out drawers to reveal their contents. To call the collection in the Toy Chest extensive wouldn't have done it justice. Some of the items were complete mysteries to her. She blinked. Several times.

"If it's too much, we can stick to the entry-level stuff. Over here." He waved to several rows in one of the chests that held standard items even she could identify. Vibrators, dildos, and a pair of fuzzy red handcuffs were visible.

Linley refused his offer of the easy way out. She shook her head and crossed to one of the more elaborate stashes of naughty paraphernalia in sealed, original packaging.

Remote controlled clitoral stimulators, electrophilia kits, and fetish equipment in every permutation were available for trial.

"Special bonus...this room comes complete with souvenirs. Three per couple. Choose wisely and you'll have toys to play with another time, or you can bronze them for posterity if I make this a night to remember." Ryder wiggled his eyebrows as he selected an enormous dildo made of sparkly blue gel. The monster had more in common with his forearm than the generous yet realistic proportions of his natural equipment.

She laughed. "Uh...no thanks."

Then something caught her eye. When the sight of the toy alone had the remnants of her climax rejuvenating, she knew it was a safe choice. Something she'd always assumed would be a great combination. Without a guy she felt comfortable enough with to ask to wear one, she'd never found out for sure.

Linley fished a small oval vibrator attached to a ring of jellied material from the top shelf. "How do you feel about this?"

"I think it's a damn good idea. The original hands-free device. Cock rings aren't necessarily my thing, but this one's practical. It'll keep the bullet in place, exactly where it counts the most while I fuck you. More orgasms for you means more of the best kind of massages for me." While he described what he intended to do, he rubbed his hand over his chest almost unconsciously, thumbing his hard nipple before following the trail of dark hair down his abdomen.

"Okay then, done." She gulped then handed him the device.

Wondering if he had any limits, Linley couldn't help herself. She plucked a leather harness complete with a hard rubber front plate and several generous penis-shaped attachments from a separate chest. When she held it up toward Ryder, he blanched a bit. A trooper, he didn't object. His shrug was slightly stiff yet he nodded. "I hadn't pegged you for a pegger. If you want to try a strap-on, I'll play along. I'm a good sport, as long as you don't spare the lube."

She grinned then set the contraption back inside the case. "I was only teasing."

"Oh, wildcat. You're going to pay for that. When you're begging to come, just remember you started it." A harsh stream of air rushed from between his parted lips followed by genuine laughter. "I like your style. Sassy. So…what else *are* you going to pick?"

Linley took a few strides to her right. She paused in front of a case she thought she understood. "Are these what I think they are?"

"If you think they're toys for anal stimulation, yes." Ryder joined her, rubbing her back in slow, calming circles. "Do you have any back door experience?"

"No." She blushed. "But I've wondered about it. We don't need toys for that though, do we?"

He rubbed against her, his thick cock riding the furrow of her ass. "Technically, no. But it's wise to start small there. Maybe take a test-drive of something modest before going for the real thing."

"Okay." She nodded. "Then how about this one? It's not too big, and it's kind of pretty."

His infectious laughter rang out again. "Only a woman would pick a sex toy on aesthetics."

"Does that mean you don't approve?" Her hand hovered over the slender stack of beads in increasing diameters that were affixed to a pliable yet stiff rubber stick.

"In no way do I object." Ryder snatched the toy from the velvet and added it to the cock ring in his hand. "And your final pick for tonight?"

"Do you have any suggestions?" She waved her hand over the row of open chests. "Something I might not have considered?"

"I know it's from the entry-level box, but some things are staples. How about one of these?" Ryder considered the row of rabbit vibrators before selecting a decent-sized model. The pale-pink shaft was filled at the base with pearls that would dance when the rotating shaft engaged.

"I had one pretty similar to it, but it sort of got worn out." She ducked her face.

"Why a woman like you has to rely on mechanics is beyond me." The pressure of his fingers on her chin nudged her face up. "But not tonight. You don't have to if you don't want to."

"It's good. And with you at the controls, I'm sure it'll be a whole new experience." The truth spilled from her easily in his presence. "It's nice to have something familiar too."

"All right then." He nodded and took their selections to the enormous bed. "Get rid of your underwear. Strip for me.

Show me what I've been dying for all night."

Linley might have been self-conscious with another man. He made it easy to forget all of her typical insecurities and flaunt her strengths. Queuing up a mental replay of the club music they'd rushed past on the main level of Underground, she gyrated her hips and began to work her panties off.

When they got past her hips, she shimmied them to the floor and stepped out of the scrap of lace.

"Brava." He clapped for her, staring at the flesh he'd tasted but hadn't had the opportunity to study. "And the bra, wildcat. Lose it."

Flicking open the clasp over her spine made her breasts thrust outward. She allowed the straps to slide from her shoulders then held the material in place, enjoying teasing Ryder. He looked as though he might start drooling any second.

When she caught sight of the heat in his stare, she put them both out of their misery.

His cock jerked when he saw her fully naked for the first time. "Spectacular."

"Thanks." Linley approached him, soaking in the heat from his gaze as it scanned her from head to toe. "Same goes, by the way."

She rested her palms on his shoulders for a second then dragged them down his chest, over his washboard abs, finally cupping his cock and balls in her palm. At least as much of him as she could hold, anyway. "Are you sure this is going to fit?"

A laugh encompassed her in its bright levity. "Yeah. We'll make it work."

"I didn't mean you in me." She squirmed as she uttered the denial. Though now that he mentioned it…he was awfully big. "I was talking about this."

Ryder moaned when she held up the cock ring. "It's

stretchy. Give it here. I'll show you."

He accepted the toy then lunged for a side table marked *Supplies*. From within a drawer he took a condom, a pair of scissors, and a bottle of lube. Then he hopped onto the bed and patted the space beside him.

It didn't take her long to comply. Snuggled up to his side, she watched as he sliced open the packaging to free her goody. Then he ripped the foil package and rolled the condom over his impressive length. Part of her sighed. She wouldn't get to feel him bare inside her. Though she took the pill and the greeter had ensured her everyone was safe, it probably wasn't proper protocol for a first hookup. *Damn.*

Once he'd sheathed himself, he flipped open the cap on the lube and squirted a dab onto his fingertip. He smeared the gel along the inside of the cock ring then stretched the material as wide as he could make it go. "Hold me still, will you?"

Like she'd decline that offer. Linley grasped his shaft around the base and pointed his cock out from his body. She loved the pulse of his heartbeat beneath her fingers.

"That might have been a strategic error," he gritted out the words. "I think I get a little bit thicker every time we make contact."

"Mmm," she purred.

With his jaw clenched, he poked the head of his cock through the ring then worked it down his length. He had to tug it past several bulges of the veins and the thickness of his shaft, but eventually the pliable material nudged her hand. She let go and allowed him to finish the job.

Expecting him to swoop in on her, she was surprised when he instructed, "Get on your hands and knees. Rest your face and shoulders on the bed. Keep your ass up high."

When she didn't comply fast enough, he smacked her ass. As if that was going to make her hurry. Hell, she might dally if that would be her reward.

"Nice try, wildcat." He chuckled. "If you wanted to be spanked, you should have opted for the Basement. Maybe next time I'll take you to the flogger room."

Linley whimpered. She wiggled her ass as she settled into the position he'd indicated. Her breasts felt heavy as they hung beneath her. If he didn't fuck her soon, she'd go nuts. Or start begging. She wasn't sure which was worse.

The distinct click of the lube opening again came an instant before something cool and smooth prodded her ass. She yelped and would have jumped, but Ryder's other hand was there, pressing between her shoulder blades, pinning her in place.

"I don't think so." He kissed the swell of her ass. "You're not going anywhere. I know you don't really want to."

"Don't tease me," she begged. "Just do this. I'm sorry I joked about the strap-on."

Ryder laughed. The sound never failed to stir her insides. "This isn't retaliation, wildcat. This is me taking care of you, whether you know it or not."

His finger pressed a bit harder on the clenched portal to her ass. He massaged lube into her, making him slide around. The sensations were powerful. More than she'd imagined. Taboo and exciting all at once.

And then he breached her resistance. His finger sank inside her. A groan burst from her chest at the simultaneous discomfort and pleasure. He continued to rub out the sting, leaving only rapture in his wake. "There you go. That's it. Focus on the good stuff."

She did as he instructed and found herself rocking back, asking for more.

Ryder withdrew instead. She cried out, uncaring about the level of her pitifulness at the moment.

"Shh." He petted her flank as the now-familiar double snap of the lube opening and shutting was followed by the press of something larger than his finger. Smoother and rounder too. This time it penetrated more easily. The bulge grew uncomfortable then slipped in just before she could object. A few seconds later he repeated the process, this time with the next larger bump.

Soon she was alternating between relieved and desperate moans.

"You're doing so well, wildcat." He nipped her ass, making her jump. "If you can handle this while I'm fucking you, maybe we'll see about graduating to something bigger, hmm?"

The swirl he added to the forward motion of the toy in her ass left her unable to reply. She figured her moans and sighs were enough affirmation.

When the base of the toy nestled into her crack, they both groaned. "You've got it all. Now hold it tight. Don't let go or I'll be disappointed. Maybe you'll get that spanking you want after all."

Linley considered intentionally disobeying him but dismissed the idea out of hand. It multiplied her pleasure to satisfy him. When he flipped her onto her back, the expression on his face left no doubt he was enjoying every second of their liaison as much as she was.

If anything, his cock jutted out farther and thicker than before, maybe courtesy of the cock ring, but she liked to think she'd had something to do with it. The manipulation of her body came easily for him, and they both enjoyed the results.

The intensity of the rhythmic clenches already pulsing within her alarmed Linley. Could she hold off long enough to shatter with Ryder?

He didn't waste any time in settling between her thighs. His cock notched in the opening to her pussy. While he covered her mouth with his and kissed her tenderly, he worked his thick cock into her channel.

The arch of her back grew more extreme as he filled her up. The heaviness of his cock parting her tissues and caressing the ache in them made her clutch him to her. Nails dug into the thick muscles of his back. Afraid to blink and miss even an instant of this amazing connection, she stared into his eyes.

He returned the fierce concentration.

Still his body moved, as if acting on pure instinct. He drilled into her over and over until the toy she'd selected nudged her clit. She moaned when it ensured every journey of his hips added the perfect stimulation to drive her closer to orgasm.

No, no, no.

She hadn't realized she'd yelled the denial until Ryder questioned her.

"I'm too close. Slow down. Give me a second. A break." She tried to stave off the impending rush.

This time his wicked grin incited a riot low in her belly. "Oh, wildcat. Now *this* is for teasing me. Hold on."

She gripped him as he flicked a remote she hadn't even noticed earlier. The vibrator strapped to him kicked in to a pleasant buzz that quickly ratcheted up to undeniable proportions. Ryder claimed her mouth, sucking on her tongue as he hammered into her. The tension in her body ensured she squeezed the beads in her ass, sending lightning bolts up her spine. The combination of stimulation was undeniable.

Linley shattered around him, hugging his cock—and the toy in her ass—over and over as she came in an endless battery of rapturous waves.

Before she'd finished shuddering, he withdrew.

"Wait." He hadn't come yet had he? Did she miss it in her complete abandon?

"No time." He flipped her over as if she weighed nothing. "Take a deep breath."

She tried through the panting that overwhelmed her as

Ryder's hand nudged her ass cheeks. The beads being tugged against her still trembling ring of muscles triggered aftershocks that felt more intense than most climaxes she'd had before tonight.

And when she was empty, he didn't waste a second before taking action to fill her up. This time she would be even fuller. He shredded the plastic housing the rabbit vibrator and used the copious fluids dripping from her pussy to insinuate it deep in her body. Flicking on both the rotation of the shaft as well as the buzz of the clit stimulator, he refused to allow her spasming body to quiet.

Just when she prepared to beg for mercy, she saw the cock ring land on the bed beside her. Her eyes widened as she realized his intentions.

"Breathe deep. Slow. Push out and let me in. Relax, wildcat." He didn't give her time to balk. Instead he fed his cock into her readied ass.

Thankfully, he was strong as hell. He kept her from thrashing and dislodging his shaft. The white-hot pain that accompanied his introduction into her virgin territory didn't last long. Though she would have reared up and smacked him away in the first instant, by the time he'd finished impaling her, the shock had turned to something decidedly more alluring.

"Jesus. You're tight and hot." He bit the intersection of her neck and shoulder as he blanketed her back. His animalistic grunts accompanied his movements within her. And before long, she lost track of everything except the complete meltdown of her inner core.

"I can feel the rabbit in you." He groaned. "It's squirming against me, through you. Feels fucking fantastic. Tell me you love this too."

"Yes!" She screamed the truth. And his name. Over and over.

Until nothing would come from her throat except for the

moans, gasps, and curses that proved he'd forced her to surrender completely to his will and the needs of her body. Another bout of ecstasy flooded her.

She imploded around Ryder.

Her ass, her pussy, her soul—no part of her remained unaffected by their encounter.

This time he allowed himself to unravel with her. He pounded into her, his big hands gripping her waist as he rose up for better leverage.

Slamming into her once, twice, more, he finally drove deep and held perfectly still. He shouted her name before a series of grunts mimicked the pulse of his cock in her ass.

Relief and euphoria mixed within her, knowing she'd granted him even a fraction of what he'd gifted her. She smiled as she let the emotions carry her away for a while.

The heat and weight of Ryder on top of her enhanced her bliss tenfold.

To find out what happened next, turn to page 147, *Ryder Epilogue.*

Chase Epilogue

Long minutes later, Linley shifted, resting on the pillows so that she faced Chase as they snuggled, replete.

"What happens now?" Afraid to ask, she choked out the question.

"Usually I fall into a deep sleep." Chase grinned. "Hope you don't mind. I'm a cuddler."

They laughed together, replete. But she couldn't shake her worry.

"No... Seriously, will I see you again?" Linley held her breath.

"I sure hope so." He kissed her lightly. "You'll break my heart if you tell me this has turned out to be the simple one-night stand you were expecting."

"It's not for you?" She didn't have his experience.

He shook his head. The intensity of his eyes convinced her it was the truth. How she'd gotten so lucky, she'd never know.

Please, please don't let real life ruin this.

"Okay then. Chase, there's something I need to tell you." She bit her lip. Pressure built in her stomach as she considered the ramifications of coming clean. But this night had meant something to her. She couldn't ignore that. Linley refused to jeopardize their future by not being straight with him upfront. Mostly upfront.

"What's wrong?" He leaned on his elbow, brushing the hair from her face.

"I'm sort of...rich."

He laughed. "That's it? Love, you're not as loaded as me I bet."

Linley didn't mean to crush his pride. "Actually, I'm the

founder and owner of Lane Technology."

"I know, *Linley*. It's an unusual name, and having Henry vouch for you didn't keep it very stealthy." He held her in place when she would have bolted. Betrayed, her stomach fell through the floor.

"You knew who I was?" She tried to block the tears of frustration welling in her eyes. It *had* been too good to be true. "The whole night?"

"Of course. I read the *Journal* every morning." Chase kissed the silvery trail of an escaping tear. "I will say your pen and ink portrait doesn't do you justice. Mine isn't very accurate either. But then again, it could never capture the spirit of the woman who's completely entranced me tonight. Plus the piece *Forbes* did on you was in the same issue they featured me. Maybe fate was trying to tell us something, Linley Lane."

"What?" She sniffled and redoubled her scrutiny of his handsome face. "You're a businessman too?"

"Kind of stings my ego that *you* didn't recognize *me*, love." He rubbed at his heart as if wounded. "I'm Chase Worthington."

This time he couldn't restrain her when she bolted upright.

"The venture capitalist?" Holy shit, he wasn't kidding. He *was* rich. The filthy, stinking, *wealthy* kind.

"At your service." He smiled. "Though you've never given me a chance to offer a partnership as you self-funded your acquisitions entirely with cash reserves. Smart. Conservative. It makes me want you again to think of your strategies in the boardroom, love."

Linley put her face in her hands and cried a tear or two of pure relief. He would understand her. Her lifestyle. Together they might be damn near unstoppable. The odds of finding him among the crowds. Impossible.

"Captains of industry... Heads of state... If Underground

is that exclusive, how is my head of security a member?"
Linley squinted at Chase.

"That's a question you're going to have to ask Henry. He
and I have been friends long enough to know he's probably
already raring to kick my ass over our liaison. At least until I
confess to him how serious it's gotten tonight, love."

"Don't you *love* me." She propped her hands on her
hips.

"Linley...I know this is crazy. And I'm not even daring
to think the *L* word after just one night but... I think you're
someone I could. You know. In time. I'm wondering..." He
closed his eyes then asked. "Will you see me again? Yes or
no?"

For Linley, there was only one option. "Yes."

The End

Ryder Loves Ties That Bind

"I requested a romp in Ties That Bind." Linley beamed when he grinned. A shiver ran through her.

"Fuck, yes." Ryder caught her off guard when he threw her over his shoulder and marched toward the fantasy chamber. He drew up short in front of the elaborately carved hardwood. When she peeked around his trim waist, she saw he paused with his hand on the knob.

"No second guessing here." She answered before he could ask. "Let's do this. Show me what's inside. I hope there's a bed, or a thick rug at least, because I need you to get me horizontal fast."

"What do you have against being fucked standing up? It can be plenty enjoyable." He grunted when she smacked his sexy ass. "Fine, feisty. I'm going."

Ryder ducked inside, closing them in darkness together. He lowered her to the ground and spun her so she faced the interior with him at her back. When he slid the dimmer up gradually, she gasped.

The room was the stuff of erotic daydreams. Gold accents offset the forest green walls. Enormous gilded mirrors reflected her stunned expression and Ryder's undivided focus on her reaction.

He smiled as she discovered the nuances of the space.

Silk scarves in every hue draped along one of the walls. The waterfall of colors and softness took her breath away. Linley wandered to the display. A board with infinite hooks, like an extended horizontal coat rack, ran along the full length of the room above the height of her head. Extravagant material hung from each.

A rainbow of dirty intentions shimmered beneath her

164

fingers as she dragged them through the luxurious fabric. It rippled in the wake of the air she disturbed as she passed. "They're beautiful. It's like a painting. Or a tapestry, I guess." Entranced, she allowed one to run through her fingers.

"Is that what you're looking for?" Ryder approached behind her, wrapping an arm around her waist. "Something soft and romantic?"

She bit her lip and turned to him. "I'm not saying that sounds like a bad idea. I'd like that sometime. But..."

"Not tonight." He nodded. "I didn't think so."

His innate understanding of her needs riled her more than the thick cock that jerked between his legs when she leaned forward to kiss his chest lightly. "Thanks."

"Come here." He took her hand and led her to a long, flat case she hadn't noticed at first. The dark, lacquered surface had hid its presence as her eyes adjusted to the space, then were distracted by the gorgeous sampling of silks.

"What is it?" She trailed a finger along the ornate inlay on top. Clearly someone prized the possessions inside.

"One of my favorite sets of gear." He might have shuddered a bit at the thought of the contents only inches below her lingering caress.

"Show me." A nod accompanied her request. If it turned him on this much, she'd like to give it a shot. As long as it wasn't something that freaked her out. The odds of that were slim given how well their desires had complemented each other all evening.

"You're a good sport, wildcat." Ryder leaned forward and kissed her deep and hard. The play of his mouth over hers rejuvenated the lingering spasms of the climax he'd gifted her with in the Downstairs common area.

"Easy when you're giving me everything I want." She brushed his smile with her thumb.

"If this is too much, you tell me." Ryder didn't move

from where his hands hovered over the latch.

"I will," she promised.

The lid didn't make the barest squeak when he lifted it. Though it seemed solid, heavy, it glided on well-oiled hinges. Inside the case, dark-red velvet made a bed for a variety of leather accessories. An array of them were lined up from shortest—at five or six inches—to longest—around four feet or so in length—in neat, parallel lines. There appeared to be pairs of each size.

"Can I touch them?" she whispered, though she couldn't have said why.

"Of course." Ryder smiled. "Do you know what they are?"

Linley's curiosity got the better of her. She selected a medium length and raised it to eye level for inspection. Heavy, stitched leather with reinforced metal rings ensured their durability, but the fur-lined insides made allowances for comfort. Butterflies launched themselves in her stomach. They flew around as she considered the possibilities. "I'm guessing it's a cuff of some sort. Right?"

The curved material fit around her forearm fairly well. Softness stroked her skin as the weight of the leather on her arm thrilled her.

Ryder smiled as he reached over. "It looks beautiful against your pale skin, wildcat. You've got it right. There is a variety of sizes to fit anyone, anywhere. Wrists, ankles, thighs, torso, hips…"

"Why would you need—?" She cut off as understanding began to dawn. "The rings… What do they attach to?"

Ryder shrugged. "It could be anything really. There are a number of hooks fastened into the structure of this room. On the walls over there. The ceiling in the center over this area rug here. And nearly infinite places on the bed. I could truss you up any way I like."

"Seriously?" Linley squeaked.

"Yes." He approached, placing another one of the cuffs around her wrist. This one fit perfectly. He latched the buckle and allowed her to wear it like a luxurious bracelet. The heft of the materials wouldn't permit her to mistake it for a frivolous bauble, though.

"What aren't you telling me, Ryder?"

For the first time that night, he hesitated. "This is your time, wildcat. It's not about me."

"It can be for us both. I thought it was." Didn't he enjoy what they'd done so far, the next level they were about to take things to?

"It has been." He was quick to reassure her. "Okay… You asked for it. These are extra chunky because they're designed to be used in suspension."

"Oh." Linley processed his admission. "You mean like—"

"Cuffing you then hanging you from the ceiling or the top of the bedframe. There's something…extra special…about seeing a woman dangling there like a ripe piece of fruit. Completely at my mercy. Trusting. Freed. Entirely helpless." Ryder swallowed hard. "Would you try that with me? It's not something I would ask of a new acquaintance except I swear this isn't like any other night I've spent with a woman I just met."

Linley nodded. "Glad to know I'm not the only one feeling that way. What the hell? I've come this far. Let's do it. If it affects you this much, I can only imagine what it'll do to me."

"I'll make sure you never forget me, wildcat." He selected the twin to the cuff on her wrist then two more, presumably for her ankles. Another seven had her canting her head, about to ask.

Ryder shook his head. "You'll see soon enough. No more talking. Get your fine ass over to that bed and get your underwear off before I've got this all set or you'll find out what it's like to be tied up and spanked."

"Is that supposed to be a deterrent?" She'd have rushed if he threatened to take away the rest of their time, not enhance the experience.

"You're going to kill me tonight." He grunted as he rummaged in the case once more.

Unwilling to defer the pleasure they practically guaranteed each other, she raced to the side of the bed, unhooked her bra and dropped it to the floor. Her panties followed close behind. She'd just kicked off the scrap of Parisian lace when Ryder plowed her over, landing on the mattress on top of her.

"Bending over in front of me like that is a dangerous maneuver, wildcat." He nuzzled her neck. "Makes me get all kinds of dirty thoughts."

"How about we save that one for some other time." She blushed when she wondered if there would be another night like this.

"Deal." He practically growled against her skin. The press of his erection in the small of her back had her wriggling beneath him until a smack of his hand stilled her. "Good girl."

Ryder rotated her, and she went willingly where he placed her. She stared up at his dark good looks, the span of his chest, and the powerful thighs bracketing her as he concentrated on securing cuffs to her various limbs. He put two sets on her arms and legs, some down low at her wrists and ankles, and a second pair at her thighs and upper arms. Then he lifted her ass to slide one beneath her and cinch it around her waist.

Two more followed, one just beneath her breasts, which he stopped to admire. Kisses and nibbles on the distended flesh of her nipples had her writhing again.

"Soon you won't have a choice but to stay where I put you." He fisted his hand in her hair and held her face still while he descended. The kiss he placed on her lips was sensual and yet steamy. She risked a love bite and was rewarded with an uttered curse.

The last attachment was a plain leather strap. He connected it to her upper arm cuffs so it ran between the two and provided a rest for her head, complete with a tiny leather pillow.

"Wouldn't want you to be uncomfortable, after all." He petted her belly, stoking the embers beginning to flame back to life.

Just when she prepared to beg him to forget all the extras and fuck her, he lunged for a nightstand marked *Supplies*. He withdrew a narrow black box along with a condom and returned to his spot between her legs in a flash.

While she licked her lips, he ripped open the foil packet and rolled the thin latex over his length with practiced ease. She wished the precaution weren't necessary, but there were only so many insane things she'd try on a first date with a guy.

"What're you laughing at, wildcat?" Ryder paused. It surprised her to catch a hint of something like vulnerability in him. Was he afraid of rejection? Judgment by friends and family? It didn't seem possible.

"Only myself." She reached for his hand and squeezed. "You're handsome. So sexy. I can't wait to feel you inside me. I was regretting that safety is necessary. Not like my usual self, I assure you."

"Ah." His devilish smirk returned. "Good to know. And thanks."

He squeezed her fingers before returning his focus to the job at hand. Now sheathed, he picked up the black box and punched a combination of buttons. Panels in the bed's canopy opened and the soft whir of motors accompanied several metal rings, which descended on the end of thin wires.

"They're mountain climbing carabineers, wildcat." He explained as he took the first and clipped it onto the metal D-ring stitched into the cuff on her ankle. "You're not going anywhere. I promise. This time we'll keep it simple. Nothing fancy to distract you. I just want you to feel what it's like to swing free while I fuck you. The rhythm of it, the weightless arc of your body crashing into mine, over and over…"

He trailed off with a groan.

By then he'd affixed a line to each of her connectors. He leaned forward to kiss her one last time then smiled. "Ready?"

"Hurry." She couldn't stand this pressure much longer. She needed him to fill her, to stretch the cramping muscles inside that drew tighter with each movement of the man who tripped every one of her crazy cravings.

Ryder clicked and held the largest button on the remote. The lines began to recede, drawing taut. Pressure built on her lower back and ribs and on her arms and legs as they began to lift from the plush bed. The instant her weight transferred entirely to the rig, she swung back and forth a bit.

She gasped, the feeling instantaneously causing a trickle of moisture to spill from her over-ready pussy.

Ryder dipped a finger into the well of her body. He embedded the digit then used his position to push her toward the headboard. It didn't take much to set her in motion. And once she swung in that gentle arc, she began to automatically fuck herself on his finger.

Though the force felt better than nothing, it only made her crave all of him.

"How's that?" He monitored her closely as if searching for any signs of panic. He could stare for another hour and never find any. Somehow, although she couldn't move or object, she finally felt completely unfettered to do absolutely nothing but enjoy the rapture he administered.

"Amazing. But not enough." She lifted her head from the

rest to stare straight into his rich chocolate eyes. "Fuck me, Ryder."

"Who am I to deny a lady?" He growled as he fisted the two wires at her hip in his grip. Her legs floated beside him as he aligned their bodies. He'd kept her just off the surface of the bed so that as he kneeled, she hovered at cock height. "You look gorgeous, wildcat."

She smiled at him then attempted to lift her hips toward him and the heavy length of his cock.

"Is this what you want?" He fisted himself then guided his hard-on to her opening. The blunt head applied significant pressure as he attempted to breach the clamping muscles of her pussy.

When he penetrated—sinking a few inches deep into her body—she first tensed then went completely limp, allowing him to possess her however he saw fit. The leather straps supporting her cradled her pliant form.

"Shit, yes." He roared as he invaded her fully.

The cords in his neck stood out, making him appear even more powerful and in control than he had before. She reeled, adoring the way he parted the tissues of her pussy and massaged her from the inside out. He impaled her on his erection then began to fuck until his balls slapped her ass and the impact of his pelvis shoved her backward.

Just like when he'd demonstrated the concept with his finger, he rocked her away then back, allowing her to fuck herself on his cock.

Linley swung like a pendulum, enjoying every glide to and fro that worked him within her from the brink of slipping free until he pressed against her cervix. After a while, she couldn't hold her head up any longer. It dropped back, and she relied entirely on the guttural sounds they both made to paint the picture of their escalating desire.

"Ryder!" She tried to warn him, but with no way to stop the intimate contact, she couldn't regulate her response.

Within seconds, she rushed toward orgasm.

"I'm there. With you. Go ahead." His hand slid from the wire and rested on her convulsing belly. A rotation of his wrist ensured his thumb rubbed her clit in irresistible circles as she rode the wave they created together away then back, over and over.

Linley's eyes flew open. She peeked up at him as she tensed then shattered.

At the same instant, Ryder shouted her name. He curled his fingers into the waistband she wore and yanked her to him tight as he pulsed within her. They ground together as they each wrung every drop of pure rapture from the experience.

Overwhelmed, Linley didn't attempt to move when he abandoned the heated mess of her pussy and carefully returned her to earth from where they'd flown together. She allowed him to work over her, admiring his sweat-sheened body as she drifted in bliss.

Once he'd sent the wires to their hiding places and removed the bands of leather from her body, he folded the covers down, tucked her inside then crashed beside her. He drew her to his chest where she listened to the pounding of his heart, which beat in sync with her own.

To find out what happened next, turn to page 147, *Ryder Epilogue.*

About The Author

Jayne Rylon is a New York Times and USA Today bestselling author. She received the 2011 Romantic Times Reviewer Choice Award for Best Indie Erotic Romance. Her stories usually begin as a daydream in an endless business meeting. Writing acts as a creative counterpoint to her straight-laced corporate existence. She lives in Ohio with two cats and her husband, who both inspires her fantasies and supports her careers. When she can escape her office, she loves to travel the world, avoid speeding tickets in her beloved Sky and, of course, read.

Jayne loves to chat with fans. You can find her at the following places when she's procrastinating:

Twitter: JayneRylon
Facebook: http://www.facebook.com/jayne.rylon
Email: contact@jaynerylon.com

Other Books By Jayne Rylon

Available Now

COMPASS BROTHERS
Northern Exposure
Southern Comfort
Eastern Ambitions
Western Ties

COMPASS GIRLS
Winter's Thaw

COUGAR CHALLENGE
Driven
Shifting Gears

MEN IN BLUE
Night is Darkest
Razor's Edge
Mistress's Master

PLAY DOCTOR
Dream Machine
Healing Touch

POWERTOOLS
Kate's Crew
Morgan's Surprise
Kayla's Gift
Devon's Pair
Nailed To The Wall

Hammer It Home

RED LIGHT (STAR)
Through My Window
Star of Christmas
Can't Buy Love
Free For All

SINGLE TITLES
Nice and Naughty
Picture Perfect
Phoenix Incantation
Where There's Smoke

IN PRINT
Cougarlicious
Dream Machine
Eastern Ambitions
Love's Compass
Mistress's Master
Needing A Cougar
Night is Darkest
Pick Your Pleasure
Powertools
Razor's Edge
Red Light
Three's Company
Watching It All
Western Ties

Coming Soon

COMPASS GIRLS
Hope Springs
Sizzlin' Summer

Falling Softly

HOT RODS
King Cobra
Mustang Sally
Super Nova
Rebel On The Run
Swinger Style
Barracuda's Heart

MEN IN BLUE
Spread Your Wings

PLAY DOCTOR
Developing Desire

IN PRINT
Love Under Construction
Two To Tango
Healing Touch

Jayne Recommends...

A Dom Is Forever
By Lexi Blake
Available Now

A Man with a Past…
Liam O'Donnell fled his native Ireland years ago after one of his missions ended in tragedy and he was accused of killing several of his fellow agents. Shrouded in mystery, Liam can't remember that fateful night. He came to the United States in disgrace, seeking redemption for crimes he may or may not have committed. But the hunt for an international terrorist leads him to London and right back into the world he left behind.

A Woman Looking for a Future…
Avery Charles followed her boss to London, eager to help the philanthropist with his many charities. When she meets a mysterious man who promises to show her London's fetish scene, she can't help but indulge in her darkest fantasies. Liam becomes her Dom, her protector, her lover. She opens her heart and her home to him, only to discover he's a man on a mission and she's just a means to an end.

When Avery's boss leads them to the traitorous Mr. Black, Liam must put together the puzzle of his past or Avery might not have a future…

Excerpt:
"I want you." She wanted him so badly. She just didn't trust that he could possibly want her.

"No, you don't, but you will." He stepped back and

tucked his shirt in. "We're going to do this my way. We tried yours and it didn't work, so I'm taking control. I should have done it in the first place. If I thought you had some, I would tell you to change into fet wear, but you don't happen to have a corset and some PVC hiding in that closet, do you?"

"I don't know what PVC is," she admitted, her heart aching a little. "I don't think this is a good idea, Lee. I don't think I can be what you need. I'm not experienced, and what experience I have wasn't very good. Don't get me wrong. I loved my husband, but the sex wasn't spectacular. I think I'm just one of those women who can't be sexy. I was trying to please you, but I couldn't."

Even in the dim light, she could see him staring, assessing. "And I think you're one of those women who can't stop thinking long enough to let her body take over. Look, Avery, the sex you've had happened with a kid. Was your husband older than you? More experienced?"

She shook her head. They had both been virgins.

"Then you have no idea what it can be like. I look at sex differently than most people. It's an exchange, and it should be good for both parties. I don't want you to spread your legs and let me have you because you want someone to hold you. If you want me to hold you, ask me. I want you to spread your legs because you can't wait another single second for my cock. I want that pussy ripe and ready and weeping for a big dick to split it wide and have its way. I want your nipples to peak because I walk into a room and you remember every dirty thing I can do to them. I want you to want me. I can make you crave me. I don't want some drive-by fucking that gets me off and I forget it five minutes later. I want to fuck all night long. I want to feel it all the next day because my cock got so used to being deep inside your body. If that's what you want, then get dressed in the sexiest thing you own and agree that I'm the boss when it comes to sex." He turned and walked out. "I'll give you five minutes to decide. I'll be waiting in your living room. If you really want me, you'll dress exactly how I've told you to dress and you'll present yourself to me for inspection. And Avery, no bra and no underwear. You won't need them."

The door closed behind him, and she had to remember how to breathe.

She wasn't sexy. She wasn't orgasmic.

But what if she could be? Lee hadn't been right about everything, but he had a few points. He'd told her he wanted to be in control and then she'd tried to make all the decisions. He had more experience, but she'd decided she knew best. She hadn't listened to him.

He wanted control. He wanted her to really want him. She didn't understand, but if she ever wanted to understand, she had to try.

She'd taught herself how to walk again. That had been an enormous mountain to climb. Why was she so scared of this? She'd faced worse, but she was cowering in her boots over not wearing underwear and a bra? She'd lost so much. Was she willing to lose this, too?

What was she really risking? She might look dumb. She could end up with her heart broken, but at least she would have proven it still worked.

She'd come across the ocean to change her life—to have a life. What was life without a few risks?

She got her phone out and sent a quick text to Adam letting him know she was home and who she was with so if she was serially murdered, at least they would have a starting place for where to find her body.

But she was going to do this because she felt safe with Lee. And because she wanted to finally understand what it really meant to want someone.

For more information, visit www.LexiBlake.net.

Made in United States
Orlando, FL
11 April 2022

16735166R00107